Marney + Me
Best Sisters 4Ever

Aleisha Gore

ISBN: 0615566200
ISBN-13: 978-0615566207

For more information please visit:
www.girlinahousebooks.com
www.marneyandme.com
www.aleishagore.com

Wishing you love!
hope! peace & strength!

DEDICATION

This book is dedicated to my sister, Shannon, my daughter, Lauri, my parents Bob and Tonya, my husband, Byron and all my friends, who believed in me from day one. Thank you for being there. Thank you for your encouragement, help and love. You give me the food for my creative soul, the only gift I need.

Love,

Aleisha

CONTENTS

Acknowledgments   vii

Part One – The Odds

1   Marney the Star   1

2   Samantha Lane Ferguson! The Brain   5

3   Fred and Jane the Parents   7

4   The Running of the Bullies   11

5   Love Those Sports Analogies   17

6   I Guess I'll Eat Some Worms   23

Part Two – Changes & Possibilities

7   Suspended   29

8   Get a Job!   33

9   All Work, No Play   37

10   Journaling   39

11   Fired   45

12   True Love   51

13   The Law of Gravity   63

14   Back to School   71

15   A Dance to Remember   73

16   Instant Replay   81

Part Three – The Law of Have & Have Not

17   Surgery and Treatment Costs Money   93

18   Crushes   99

19   In the Papers   101

Part Four – If You Want Something Bad Enough

20   Back in the Game   107

21   Generous Doctor Mackey   111

22   Growing Up   115

23   The Long Road Home   119

24   To Be or Not To Be Handicapped   129

25   Cong's Mom   131

26   Report Card Day   135

Part Five – Heroes

27   Marney the Hero   143

28   Sam the Hero   147

29   Mom & Dad the Heroes   151

     About the Author   155

     Author's Glossary   159

ACKNOWLEDGMENTS

Special Thanks to:
Henry Tuason for the cover photography
and
Michaela Haas and Megan Palmer
for being the perfect cover models.

And to YOU, dear Reader.
I want you to know that this book is for you- a gift from me to tell you that if things are looking tough, you've got me. Just open up this book and read the story of Sam and Marney, written just for you...

I hope you smile.

Aleisha Gore

Part One – The Odds

1 MARNEY THE STAR

The roar of the crowd was the last thing Marney heard before it happened. She got hit. Hard.

One year ago, my sister, Marney, was the star athlete of her entire school, maybe even in the entire universe. She's always been the star of my universe.

Marney played basketball and she did it with so much life that even people who were completely uninterested in basketball went to the games to see her play. She was voted Most Valuable Player in her Freshman, Sophomore and Junior year of High School. Now in her Senior year, the stakes are higher because of that one fateful game.

It was a very tight game. At the end of each quarter, one side trailed, then they'd come back and the other side trailed. At fourth quarter with mere seconds to go, the game was tied 48-48. The Dragons were fired up and getting ready to knock us, the Diamondbacks, right out of our skins!

I heard Marney call out, "We're the home team. We can't go down without a fight!"

The team jumped into action, like she'd breathed life back into them. She has a way with people and a way of igniting their spirit of involvement and enthusiasm even if she's not that great of a wordsmith. They follow her and I think they'd follow her to the end of the universe.

1

The referee blew the whistle to signal the last timeout was up. It was time for the Diamondbacks to strike or to fall.

Instinctively, I knew Marney couldn't lose. She wouldn't let that happen.

As the clock began its final countdown, the spectators began to shout.

"Six! Five!"

Marney ran down the court with such speed and agility, I think people on the benches thought they were watching a precision dance. She dribbled the ball left and right like a boxer dodging a punch.

"Four! Three!" the fans mimicked the clock.

With nimble steps, she avoided a steal, and passed to a teammate.

"Two!"

Steadfast and nowhere to go but up, Marney flew like Supergirl up to the net when her teammate threw the ball back to her.

"One!"

She slam dunked it. Buzz.

The sound of the buzzer competed with the cheers of the wild crowd and all the while Marney's world went in slow motion. Once the ball was sunk, no one noticed the player who, surely by accident, changed Marney's life for good.

Marney had been hit. A girl on the opposing team had run into her as she dropped down from her flying dunk. Marney flew backwards toward the gazers and photographers court side. As Marney came crashing down a snap in her back quelled every other commotion. The crowd's cheers were muffled by a common gasp.

When the opposing player got up off her, Marney didn't get up. She couldn't get up.

Later, the doctor said she was lucky; that if the crowd sitting court side hadn't broken her fall, she would've received a more severe spinal injury, losing the use of everything from her neck down instead of just her legs.

Marney has been wheelchair bound since that day. It was the day that, for some miraculous reason, changed Marney's life but it never changed her attitude.

She still plays basketball. She's not a Diamondback anymore, she's a Challenger and she plays wheelchair basketball. It's different, harder, I think, but she still knocks them dead. It's like she never stopped even though it seemed her life did. She also wants to attend a big university.

She may have to go out of state so she can go somewhere where they have a girl's wheelchair basketball team. I think there are only seven of those in the United States and Canada. But, I'd be devastated if she left home. I know life doesn't revolve around me. But we have to stay Best Sisters Forever. Can we do that if she's away? I've heard long distance relationships don't last. Where am I going to get my sisterly advice from if she's gone?

I remember she told me that because of what happened to her, I had no excuse for failing.

"I'm failing because I'm bored and lazy. I'm not stupid." I told her.

Marney pulled a book out of her back pocket and read something to me.

"You like to read?" I mocked her.

She's still more of a jock than a scholar. But, she had a point.

"Shut up, Squirt. This is important."

She pointed to the book.

"It's from an important man in history. Winston Churchill. He says, 'Never, never, never, never give up.'"

I learned that day, without her telling me, that it wasn't just life she wasn't giving up on. I learned she would never give up her legs.

"You shouldn't give up either, Squirt."

I felt a lecture coming on.

"If you're bored, you need to talk to the school counselors again to give you classes that you're interested in, that you're excited about, something that you can learn."

When had Marney grown up anyway?

"I'm a seven year old, in the seventh grade, Marney! Don't you think they know I'm a genius and need something to stimulate my mind?"

She threw the book at me. She's not all grown up yet.

"You know what I mean. Do something."

She held her hand out. I picked the book up from the floor and handed it to her.

She began to roll away and then said, "You're such a brain. But when do you use it?"

2 SAMANTHA LANE FERGUSON! THE BRAIN

I'm a genius. I'm not trying to be big headed or toot my own horn. I really am a genius.

In Kindergarten, I was obviously out of place when I started reading the newspaper the teacher left on her desk.

In the first grade, I was doing complex math, reading Shakespeare and writing Haikus.

That's when the counselors at the school told my parents they should have me tested. My parents agreed to the tests and I was tested. I tested past five grade levels and instead of going into the second grade, I went into the seventh.

With "all them smarts" I ought to be able to think of something good to do.

Because I'm small for my grade, Marney has nicknamed me Squirt. I like it. At school, they just call me The Brain. I like that, too. It makes me feel like I'm going to take over the world.

Even though Marney's my big sister, she treats me like I'm her kid. It's kind of ironic, since I treat Mom and Dad like they're family friends. I call them by their given names, Jane and Fred. They call me, Samantha Lane Ferguson! although I'm fairly certain my birth certificate doesn't contain the exclamation point. I am thinking of adding it though.

Can I really help it? I'm in the seventh grade and my exceptionally large vocabulary has increased its catalog of four letter words. I remember the first time I said a magical four letter word in front of Fred and Jane.

"Samantha Lane Ferguson!" They screamed out in unison. Sometimes I could swear they were Siamese twins.

I didn't say that four letter word again, in front of them, anyway.

In the seventh grade, kids say it a lot. I get the impression, they think it sounds cool. Being that I am the new kid in school and just happen to be five whole years younger, I sometimes feel the need to go with the flow. But Fred and Jane don't seem to understand that. What they label as an opportunity, for the most part, I see as a nightmare.

The kids here are a full two feet taller than me. On my first day, some kid asked me if I was lost. Another just stared at me as I tried to open a locker, which was almost my same height.

When they realized I was actually a student, a few of them pretended to like me so they could copy my homework. I think that's when I decided to stop doing it. Plus, sometimes it's just so monotonous. I need some stimulation. Something exciting. I need basketball for the mind. I honestly don't know why I have to do homework anyway. I do just fine on the tests.

But, some of the teachers, especially Mrs. Margott says, "That's not the point. You need to do the work."

Oh brother.

3 JANE AND FRED THE PARENTS

Do I have brothers?

No.

I kind of wish I did. But, I have Jane and Fred and I have Marney.

I think Marney secretly thinks it's hilarious that I call our parents Jane and Fred.

She told me the story of when I was a baby and I started talking (which was a lot earlier than most babies talk, too.) I was three months old and Fred was trying to get me to say "Daddy." Jane wanted me to say, "Mommy." Marney made it out to be some kind of competition. Which word would I say first?

When "Fred" came out, Marney laughed out loud.

Fred said, "I won. She said 'Dad.'"

Marney chuckled again and informed him otherwise.

"No, she didn't, Dad. She said, 'Fred.'"

Then she tried to suppress another laugh.

"I'm sure she said, 'Dad.'"

Jane tried to reassure him.

But, then the defining moment came. I said it again and this time, there would be no mistaking it.

"Fred!"

I called his first name out loud and then blew spit bubbles.

Marney burst out laughing. She was ten years old.

She picked me up, said, "See, I told you so," and took me to her room to show me her sports posters.

I think that's when Jane and Fred realized Marney and I were just enough kids for them.

The next word I learned was "Jane" and then "Marney" and then "basketball." Marney really liked that.

She watched TV sports and went to games and as soon as she was old enough, she signed up for a team. Fred was there every step of the way. Since he didn't have a son, a tomboy would serve his needs to bond with a sports loving fanatic any day.

Jane didn't seem to mind it either. I guess she thought that since she still had one girl left she could try to mold me into a princess. Those plans were dashed when I'd refused to wear the pretty froufrou dresses she put me in. Once she managed to actually put me in one and I disappeared. I heard her calling my name, looking for me. When she finally found me, I was outside near the side of the house, sitting in a bucket, filled with water, the hose still running. She finally stopped buying them for me.

Still, maybe every once in a while or on a really special occasion, like when Marney graduates, I will wear a dress and make Jane happy. Maybe.

Jane works as a secretary for Fred's general contractor business. Their business used to pay the bills and the mortgage but since Marney's accident, I noticed the stack of overdue notices are getting bigger. When the hospital's billing department calls, sometimes Jane won't answer the phone. I've heard Fred and Jane argue about what to do about it, especially since Marney wants to go to a university.

Kind of ironic, isn't it, that such ordinary people bore such special kids?

4 THE RUNNING OF THE BULLIES

There's a boy at school and I know Marney said to use my brain, but I like him. He's cute. Even the girls in the bathroom think so.

"He's so hot," I overheard them say.

I'm sure it's a little ridiculous to think that a 12-year-old boy would even think twice about a 7-year-old. But maybe in ten years. Ugh! Ten years is a long time. What if he changes by then? What if he's not even cute anymore? What if he's covered in hair? Oh, why do I have to be a 7-year-old genius?

"Oh, why can't I be a twelve-year-old dumb blond?"

"What did you say?" demanded the girls in the bathroom while peeking into my stall and banging on the door.

I guess I must have said that last thought out loud because suddenly, my bathroom stall was surrounded by 12-year-old girls tapping their shoes on the tile floor. I had nowhere to go. So, I opened the stall.

"Uh, do you mind if I wash my hands?"

I walked through them toward the sinks while they huffed and puffed. I washed my hands and ignored their glares drilling into the back of my head.

"I said, I wish I were a twelve-year-old dumb blond," I stated matter-of-fact.

The girls didn't seem that impressed by what I was saying, so I went on to clarify my stance on the issue.

"Come on, you've been my age before. The only difference between you and me is I'm small and you're big. We basically have the same needs. We want the same things."

The girls in the bathroom looked perplexed. So, I continued, pacing the room like an attorney pleading my case.

"For example, we both want to pass the seventh grade. We both want to make friends and we both..."

I couldn't stall much longer and I didn't know what to say next.

"I like a boy in school and he doesn't even know I'm alive. I thought if I was bigger here, here and here," pointing to my height, flat chest and butt, "and less of a nerd, he might like me."

The girls looked at each other and laughed hysterically. Then as they made the capital L sign on their heads with their thumbs and index fingers, they walked out talking about me as if I wasn't even there.

I didn't find it funny. Being small in a big kid's world is like being surrounded by ice cream and having a milk allergy, cute boys everywhere and not one under 12 years old. I kept trying to reassure myself that when I was a baby these adolescents were only 5-year-olds. That's not a huge age difference and, by the way, when I'm 18, they'll only be 23 and when I'm 40, they'll be 45.

I slunk out of the bathroom hoping to avoid all signs of pubescent life. No such luck. The girls had gathered the pack and started the telephone game, complete with nasty words, rumors and all sorts of distorted notions to make me the gazelle in a hallway full of lions. I stood there frozen. They began to tease me.

"The Brain wants a boyfriend."

I don't like teasing. I blame Jane and Fred. Why did they have to have me tested? I should have been in the 2nd grade right now teaching green-nosed little kids how to do multiplication. I'd have ruled that school and I would've felt good about myself. Right now, all I want to do is die. At least that was one thing we could all agree on.

Seventh grade girls are ruthless animals. I didn't know if I was going to leave the hallway in one piece. It seemed like an eternity that I stood there and that they stood around me mocking me. I tried to make them all fade away and think of a happy place. I noticed Fred does that when Jane is nagging him. It worked for a moment. Then the bell rang and as the saying goes, I was saved.

The kids separated and moved in the direction of their various classes. The leaders of the pack turned in unison, arm in arm, and walked toward their class. I looked at myself from top to bottom-- not a scratch. I had survived this time. But, I had a feeling this fight wasn't over yet.

I was right. After school, there were some girls waiting for me at the entrance. Marney usually picks me up right where they were standing. I slowly walked toward them hoping that they'd disperse before I got there. I looked around for a supervising adult and was, once again, disappointed. There was another spot where I could wait and Marney should be able to see me just fine. As I walked past the group of girls, one of them held their arm out to grab me and pull me back in.

"Hi!" I stated enthusiastically, but my big scary-looking grin slowly faded.

"What are you, like, a midget or something?" one of the girls asked me and then pulled out a lollipop from her pocket and opened it. The others laughed.

I corrected her, "I thought I explained this before. I skipped a few grades and now I'm here."

The girl put the lollipop in her mouth. The other girls were chewing gum and maybe it's the daredevil in me or maybe it was just stupidity, but I said something that made them very very angry.

"Did you know that in German, the word, cow, means to chew? Not really spelled the same but still."

"Are you, like, calling us cows?" another girl asked.

All three girls gathered closer to me, huddling me in a tight circle. Looking up at their faces, they really did look like cows. I'm glad I don't like chewing gum. One of the girls, who I thought, was really big, even for her age, began to pick me up. This was one of those times I really wished I wasn't so smart. She picked me right up and put me into the trash can a few feet away. What's worse is that Marney rolled up to meet me right at that moment. But it was too late. She couldn't have saved me anyway. The girls ran off laughing and I had been placed not ever so delicately onto something very smelly and sticky. They'd won--this time.

Marney rolled up to the trash can and I tried to boost myself up so she could pull me out. But, she couldn't manage. Suddenly I saw him, Dean Marlowe, he was there beside Marney and me and he reached into the trash can, grabbed my arms and pulled me out. My hero.

"Thanks Mr. Marlowe," I said to him.

Mr. Marlowe's our phys-ed teacher. He's super cute and all the girls at school like him. His is the only class I had an "A" in.

It appeared I wasn't the only one who thought Mr. Marlowe was cute. Marney was looking at him with a look I've never seen before. She was blushing.

"Marney, this is Mr. Marlowe. He's our P.E. teacher."

Mr. Marlowe held out his hand to Marney. She took it absentmindedly and still didn't speak.

"Mr. Marlowe, this is my sister Marney."

"Hi!" Mr. Marlowe said loudly. "It's nice to meet you! Your sister's a good kid."

I laughed.

"Mr. Marlowe, she's not deaf. She just can't use her legs. Everything else works."

I took aim at Marney who now looked like a deaf mute.

"Marney!"

I kicked her leg and then I was sorry. I knew Marney didn't feel it, but she didn't like her legs being messed with either.

"Sorry Marney."

Marney, embarrassed and upset, spoke up, "We gotta go. Nice talking to you."

Mr. Marlowe stood there and waved goodbye.

"Sorry Marney. I forgot," I plead.

"It's okay, Squirt. It's not your fault."

She was still self-conscious about her legs. It's kind of strange to have something there that you can see and touch but not feel or use.

"Your P.E. teacher was really cute."

"Oh, I hadn't noticed," I laughed.

She laughed too, then asked, "So, what happened with those girls?"

"I called them dumb blonds."

Marney laughed at me.

"I mean, I didn't do it directly. But somehow it was directed. Oh, and I called them cows."

Marney laughed again.

"Again, not directly."

Marney looked at me and gave me another noogie, "You have a way of directly getting yourself in trouble, don't you?"

I smiled at her. "That's okay Marney. I've got you to bail me out."

Marney smiled back and kept rolling home.

5 LOVE THOSE SPORTS ANALOGIES

As Marney rolled along with me seated in her lap, we talked about school. Since she's "in the twelfth grade now, things are going to change,"she said.

Secretly, I knew what she was talking about but I asked, "How?" I liked it when she explained things to me. She had an interesting way of looking at everything from a kind of sports point of view.

"Well, Squirt, you know I'll be going away to college, and I may not be around that much. I may even have to go out of state for college."

"But Marney," I replied, "I need you. You can't leave."

"It won't be for that long and you know what?" she reassured me, "I'm here now. So, if there's anything you want to talk about, I'm all ears."

Since I'm in the 7th grade, I do what most other 7th graders do. I put on makeup, with some difficulty here and there and everywhere. And I talk about boys. Okay, I listen about boys. So, there's a lot I wanted to talk about with Marney.

"I went to pee today and while I sat on the toilet, those girls came in and smoked cigarettes and talked about boys."

"Yes?" She asked.

So I went on. "They talked about boys and girls kissing and who liked who and they also talked about boobs and who's got the biggest ones--When will I get boobs?" I must have been talking a hundred miles a minute because she asked me to slow down.

"Slow down. Don't grow up so fast, Squirt." She spoke to me in an out-of-breath kind of way. She was still pushing that wheelchair. It was not electric. She purposely didn't want that. "It'll make me lazy and depressed and then I won't play," she said about it. That was that.

"But you said, 'never slow down.'" I retorted.

"That's different," she explained. "When you're young you want to be older and when you're older you want to be younger. Just enjoy your time, your childhood."

"I'm not a child." I held my arms together and huffed.

She just smiled. "You know, life is like a basketball game..."

I love her sports analogies.

She continued, "You start out with a lot of time on the clock and as time goes by, you get tired. But, it's still fun if you play it right and if you don't overexert yourself to the point of injury."

I really admired her insight right then and there. She was everything I needed a big sister to be.

When we got home, she made me a peanut butter and banana sandwich and we sat in the living room watching The Simpsons. Hanging out with Marney made me forget all about the bullies at school, especially since Bart Simpson made school bullies look so dumb. "Eat my shorts!" He made me laugh. But, we couldn't watch for too long because Marney doesn't like to stay still for long periods and plus Jane would be coming home soon.

Jane didn't like it when I ate my sandwiches without a plate. I always dropped crumbs on the floor. I heard the car coming up the driveway and quickly picked up the crumbs. Marney went into her room and closed the door. I unloaded my backpack and threw the books on the table, opened up my math book and took out my homework. I started filling out the problems as quickly as I could and then she walked in. Phew!

"Oh good, you're doing your homework," Jane said.

I smiled at her, "Yep."

"You need any help?" she asked.

"Nope," I responded.

"Of course not," she replied.

I suddenly got angry. "Well, it's not my fault that I'm so smart, Jane!"

Jane gasped. She hated when I said it. It wasn't a term of endearment like Mommy would have been and I think she resented me.

"Sorry."

Jane composed herself and walked over to me and hugged me. "It's okay Samantha. Mommy's just had a hard day. That's all."

I realized that adult hard days are far harder than kid hard days so maybe Marney's got a point with that basketball analogy. But what do they expect me to do? I'm in the 7th grade and people are talking about sex. We're even going to learn Sex Ed this year. Maybe they'll talk about boobs.

"Here Jane," I handed her a form from health class. "You have to sign this and I have to bring it back tomorrow."

Jane took the paper and looked at it. She seemed to get really flustered about it. "Um, Samantha. Did you read this already?"

"Yes, of course," I stated boldly.

"You know I can't sign this," she replied with a prudish eyebrow lift.

"But, it's part of the class. I have to do it. It's health," I reasoned.

She shook her head, "No, you don't have to do it. There's an opt-out line here and we are opting out," she stated while finishing signing the opt-out. "You can go to the library when they hold that part of the class. You won't be marked down, they'll give you a separate project."

"I know. I read it," I replied with disappointment.

Marney came into the room then. "You thought you could get away with it, eh, Squirt?" She chuckled. "Can't pull the wool over Mom's eyes." She rubbed my head with her fist. I hated noogies. They made my hair stand on end.

Jane looked at Marney, "Speaking of eyes, why are yours so red, Marney?"

I looked at Marney. "Have you been crying?"

Jane looked at me and then back at Marney. The room had gone silent as a black hole.

"Oh! Forget about it," Marney stated angrily. She wheeled herself back to her room.

"Don't you want dinner?" Jane called out.

"I'm not hungry," Marney yelled back and slammed the door.

Later on, I heard Jane and Fred talking. "Could she be smoking pot?" I heard Fred ask.

"Not a chance. Our daughter? We raised her right." Jane responded.

"You're probably right. Besides who am I kidding? She's a sports junkie," Fred reasoned.

It's hard to believe the truth when I or anyone else just observes her because she's so enthusiastic and cheerful, in general.

"Then what could be wrong?" Fred asked.

"I hate to think that my daughter is depressed. But maybe that's what it is, Fred. Do you think the accident has finally gotten to her?" Jane made a grand observation, but it was still a little off.

The accident hadn't finally gotten to her. It always had gotten to her, from day one. I put together the clues I had seen over the last year. I remembered hearing crying coming from her room. I remembered hearing videos playing. One day, I snuck in there to see what she'd been watching. Her playlist on youtube was filled with videos of her basketball games from before the accident. She missed her legs. They were there but they weren't. She watched the videos to feel them there again.

I'll keep her secret and take it to the grave. Until the day she decides she wants me or anybody, for that matter, to know about it, I cross my heart. I shall not speak a word.

6 I GUESS I'LL EAT SOME WORMS

I hate school. There, I said it. It was boring before, but now it's just horrid and I hate it. Why should I even have to go? Why can't I just stay home teaching myself online for five years until I'm old enough to fit in? That would make sense to me. Today was the worst day of my life. I want to stay home forever.

The morning started out okay. But as soon as lunch rolled around, I was back in the sights of the wild animals. Strange how one wrong move can make everything go wrong. Today was that kind of day.

I sat at the table with my regular group of friends, if I can call them that, the uncool kids, the smart kids, the both uncool and dumb kids, and any other riff-raff who was willing to sit with both the smartest and the youngest kid in school. All of the sudden, they all, every single one of them, scattered like cockroaches. I looked up and what to my very eyes should appear? The bathroom girls. My bathroom eaves dropping days were over. If God let me out of this one, I would raise my right hand and swear it.

"I told you, it wasn't over," the pack leader said.

"I know, and then your friend, Mongo put me in the trash can."
Oh, why do I continuously put my foot in my mouth and regret it?

Mongo looked at me and growled. I swear I could see fangs. Was this girl really in the 7th grade? She looked like she was in high school.

"I don't think you're hungry today, little Munchkin."

The pack leader grabbed my food and handed it to Mongo. Mongo promptly ate it. The pack leader smiled.

"Every day, you will bring us your lunch."

"Aren't you worried about getting fat?"

There I go again. What's with me?

"Every day you will bring us your lunch," she gritted her teeth as she repeated herself. Then she grabbed my arm by the wrist.

It hurt. I couldn't believe it. I've heard of bullying like this but never knew it actually 000existed. This was really hands-on. This was bigger and badder than being shoved in a locker or dropped in a trash can. This was abuse. Her grip became tighter.

"You won't say a word to your mommy and daddy."

She finally let go.

The pack turned and walked away with attitude in their step. I looked down at my wrist. It was bright red and turning purple. I had been assaulted. The sarcastic clown inside me had just suffered a knockout and what was happening now? What's this? Tears began to stream down my face. Oh no, this can't happen. I ran out of the cafeteria and as I neared the bathroom, I knew I had no safe place to hide. No place to hide my tears. Instead I ran right out of the school, right past the truancy officer and jumped onto a city bus heading homeward.

When I got home, I ran to my room and let out enough sobs that even I was feeling sorry for myself. What a fool. Thank goodness no one was home. I could cry all I wanted and I could kick the door, the chair, the table leg, my book bag, the wall--anything I wanted and no one would know. I could let it out and I did.

Jane, Fred and Marney got home really late and it was all because of me. When Marney showed up at the school and I was nowhere to be found, not even the trash cans, she called Fred and Jane and all of them went out looking for me. They even went to the police station. All of them were in tears when they got home but that changed when they saw me. Their tears at first turned to relief and joy as they grabbed and hugged me and then to anger.

"Where the hell were you, Young Lady?" Fred demanded.

Marney looked at me with her arms crossed. Jane rubbed tears out of her eyes.

I answered softly, "I've been home since lunch. I took a bus."

Jane asked, "Why on earth would you do that?"

I was holding my wrist so no one could see the mark, but it was hard to miss.

"I got bullied again at lunch and I couldn't stay there. I couldn't." Tears began streaming out of my eyes again.

Marney wheeled herself over to me. She grabbed my arm and held it up. "What the----."

"Marney!" Jane interrupted. "Don't you dare say it."

"Ok Mom, but do you see her wrist? I'm gonna kick someone's butt tomorrow."

"Oh no!" I told Marney. "Don't do anything, please."

Jane and Fred looked at my wrist. They were really angry.

"Who did this to you Samantha?" Fred asked.

I stayed silent.

"Samantha? You need to tell us so we can talk to the principal and the kid's parents. This is bad."

Because I didn't speak up, Marney jumped in.

"Mom, Dad, I'll handle it. I'll go down to the school tomorrow and talk to the principal." Marney reasoned, "I think Samantha would be okay with that. Wouldn't you, Squirt?"

I nodded. It was better than Jane and Fred coming to the school. I would be so embarrassed. It's bad enough to be bullied, but when your parents come to the school, the bullying goes up to a whole new level.

Part Two – Changes & Possibilities

7 SUSPENDED

I t's official, 7th grade must be the 7th circle of hell. Marney hates me. I'm public enemy number one by the principal's standards and there's still a pack of mean girls after me at school.

Today Marney arrived with me at the school just as she promised Jane and Fred she would. But instead of everything coming up roses, Marney made her own life much more complicated.

When Marney went to the principal with my complaint, the principal stated that nothing could be done because it was my word against the other girls' and since it would end up being a "she said, she said" kind of thing, that it would be best to leave it alone. "Give it some cooling off time," she insisted.

Marney was not happy about this and rolled angrily out of the principal's office, letting the door slam. I was pretty proud of her, but then the trouble really began.

The wild animals were in the hall after a long smoke in the bathroom. I could smell their Marlboro perfume. I got really close to Marney as we walked toward the exit and down the hall.

She asked, "What's the matter?"

She looked at me. She looked at them. They looked at me.

"That's it," she said and she rolled over to the girls.

I was surprised. They were even more surprised. She was twice as big as them even in the wheelchair--she looked scary.

"What do you want, Roller-bitch?" the pack leader asked Marney. The girls laughed and gave each other high-fives. Marney was seeing red.

"You lay a finger on my little sister again and I'll roll you, all right, I will roll you up into a little ball, dribble you and throw you through a basket."

Then Marney grabbed her arm. "You got that?"

Everyone gasped, including me.

"Excuse me?!" the principal called out while walking toward them.

"Oh no," I said to myself.

Marney let the girl's arm go. The girl stood eagerly in front of the principal and pretended to be innocent.

The principal demanded,"How dare you?"

"Principal Grey, this lady grabbed me!" the pack leader whined like a little girl.

I kind of smiled. I knew Marney was going to get punished for this, but I couldn't help but think how great it was that someone finally scared this bully as much as she scared me. Still, what happened next couldn't be justified by my satisfaction.

"Ms. Ferguson, you are lucky you are not eighteen yet, otherwise you could be arrested for assault. Come into my office."

Marney and I went back into the principal's office. I worried now the principal really would call the police. She picked up the phone. Instead she dialed Jane. Jane was not happy. Then she dialed Marney's school. Marney's principal told her coach and the coach suspended Marney from the next six games at school. The principal suspended her from school for a week. By the time we left that office, Marney was in the dog house and I didn't have a friend in the world, not even Marney.

When I got home, I threw my books across my room.

"Oh, why did I have to be so smart?" I yelled into the mirror.

A knocking at my door, made me turn to look. Fred walked into my room, took me in his arms and patted my head.

"Samantha, you have a lot to learn about yourself and others. And it's a good thing you're smart. Not a bad thing."

"Marney hates me."

"Marney doesn't hate you," he answered back. "She's just upset and she'll get over it."

"Six games, Fred." I told him.

"I know," he said. "She'll find something to do. Maybe you two can find something to do together."

"She's seventeen, Fred."

Marney was mad at me. I could tell. At dinner, she barely looked at me. And hardly anyone spoke. But Fred had a few ideas about what to do with her free time. Afterward I asked her if she wanted to go outside and shoot hoops together.

She said, "I've got better things to do then play games with you, Samantha."

She never calls me Samantha.

8 GET A JOB!

Tonight at dinner, Fred told Marney that as long as she was suspended from school and wasn't going to be playing any games for a while that she had to get a job to help the family out with some extra cash.

Marney wasn't too happy about that but I guess she didn't put up much of a fuss since she really doesn't have anything else to do but feel sorry for herself.

She went to the school's website and applied to jobs listed in the job center. I wanted to see if I could help.

"Marney, I can help. I can run down to the yogurt shop and ask for an application. That way if you get a job there, you can give me a discount."

I laughed. Marney didn't. She wasn't at all responsive to my help. But, I did it anyway.

The next day, I went into the guidance counselor's office at the school to ask if she knew of any jobs. As I sat there waiting for her, I noticed there were all sorts of interesting fliers. I saw information on a new church that's coming to our neighborhood. Maybe they will help me and tell me how I can make Marney not be so mad at me. I also took a flier for a doctor that maybe would be good for Marney's condition.

When the guidance counselor saw me, she asked me what I needed all the fliers for. I told her that Marney was mad at me and I didn't want her to be mad so I needed to make it up to her somehow.

Then I told her "I'm also looking for a job."

"You have to be fifteen to get your work permit, Samantha," she said.

"Not for me. I'm just a kid," I told her. "I already have enough on my plate without having to worry about a job."

When I got home from school, Marney had already lined up an interview with a grocery store down the road. I guess that wouldn't be too bad. She could do pretty much everything that any other employee without a handicap could do except reach tall shelves. I thought it could be a good thing. But, I still gave her the application for the yogurt shop.

"Here you go, Marney." I handed it to her with all the other stuff I got from the counseling office.

"What's all this?" she asked me.

"I was just thinking of things we can do and well, places that maybe you could take me," I replied.

"What's this?" She showed me the flier from the doctor.

"That's a doctor," I answered.

"Yeah, and what's his flier doing in my hand?"

"I thought we could go see him. He's giving a talk. Maybe you want to go?"

"What for?"

I couldn't believe she was acting like this. It totally was not like her.

"His talk is on spinal surgery and there will be people there--in wheelchairs--people like you. Hello?"

Marney looked angry, "No one is like me. No one."

Fred popped his head in my room.

"Stop feeling sorry for yourself and go with your little sister. She cares about you Marney."

"Dad?" she said, "personal space."

"Yeah, Fred, my room," I agreed.

"Oh. Right," Fred answered.

Marney looked at me, I looked back at her and she smiled. I smiled back. She rolled over to me.

"Ok, Squirt. Maybe we'll go."

She gave me a noogie. Ah! I hate noogies. But, I was very glad she was talking nicely to me again. It's much easier being a genius with a handicapped sister. Then, I'm not the only special one.

9 ALL WORK NO PLAY

A couple days later, Marney found out, she didn't get the job at the store, but she did take the application into the yogurt shop and they interviewed her, too. She did so well, they gave her the job on the spot.

"Hallelujah!" Jane said.

I have never heard Jane say that before. Marney was pretty happy about it, too. She likes to be busy. It's only temporary until she gets back onto the team, but that's okay. She's happy, so I guess I'm happy. Maybe I can still go over there and hang out sometimes. I love frozen yogurt, and besides I'll do all I can to spend time with my big sister. After all, she's the only one I have.

"Marney, you wanna go to the park and shoot some hoops?" I asked her.

"No, Squirt. I gotta go to work."

"Can I go with you to work?"

"No."

"I won't bother you."

"No."

"I'll be quiet."

"No you won't."

"I'll try to be quiet."

"No you won't, Squirt, and I wouldn't ask you to either."

Marney rolled over to me and patted me on the head.

Well, it didn't take long to figure out I did not like work. They took Marney away from me and now we are never going to see each other except right before bed. I am not so happy about this anymore. Why   did   she   have   to   get   that   job?

10 JOURNALING

Today our English teacher gave us each a journal and said we must make an entry every day. It doesn't matter when, during school, out of school, whenever, as long as it's every day and at the end of each week we need to turn in the journals to be inspected for grading. Now, that's something I can do. Marney will be very proud of me. I'm finally doing my homework. It's easy too because we have journal topics and we have to use one each time. Piece of cake.

Journal Topic #1   I'd like to say a good thing about----

Dear Journal,

I'd like to say a good thing about journaling. I think journaling will be fun and inspire me to do something. Maybe Ms. Harper will be happy that I'm finally doing classwork. My sister Marney always says she wants me to do something with my life. This could be a good place to start.

Marney is my sister but she's also my best friend. I haven't had a friend, a real friend, since I left school last year. I depend on her. Just the other day, she got a job and I am really scared about it. She works all the time after school now, so I don't get to see her so much.

I'm not that close to my parents because they're not like me. I'm not like them. I sometimes feel like I'm not like anybody.

Love,
Sam

Journal Topic #6 When people get angry they should----

Dear Journal,

When people get angry they should write to their senator or their parents or to their teachers, whoever they are mad at or whoever is in charge of the situation they are mad about. I realize this is something I should do now. Because I'm angry. If I was angry about war, I would write to the president. But I'm angry about other things.

I am angry about Marney's accident. I'm angry about the bills piling up on Fred and Jane's desk which make them angry and I'm angry about Marney getting a job which takes her away from me. I'm also angry that at lunch today they didn't have any chocolate dessert left. I feel cheated. I paid the same amount as everyone else and I didn't get the dessert, which means one of two things: they either didn't order enough or they gave someone extra. Favoritism makes me angry too. Maybe I should write to the principal.

Love,
Sam

I wrote a letter to Jane and Fred and told them how I felt about them arguing:

Dear Jane and Fred,
I don't like it when you argue.
Please stop.
Love,
Sam
P.S. I also don't like that Marney has to work. I am lonely.

I left the letter on the kitchen stove where Jane would see it as soon as she walked in the door. She always goes to the kitchen as soon as she gets home because she needs to cook right away. Which reminds me, I wonder what Marney eats now that she's not home for dinner.

Like clockwork, Jane got home and she must have been switched on like a robot because before she knew it, she'd turned the stove on, lighting my letter on fire and burning half of it before she even woke up out of her daily routine.

"Samantha Lane Ferguson!" was what I heard next.

I ran into the kitchen.

Jane was holding up a half burned letter. "What is this?" she asked me.

"It's a letter."

"I know it's a letter. What's it doing here on my stove?" she demanded.

"I knew you'd find it there. It was important and I wanted you to see it right away," I replied innocently.

"Samantha, you've got to think." She knocked her fist on her head. I really hate that. It makes me feel stupid. Who's the genius here, anyway?

"Well, how the hell was I supposed to know you would burn it instead of reading it?" I said, not so innocently.

"Samantha! Do not use that tone with me, Young Lady. It just so happens, I did read it."

She read it. Just the paper got burned not the words. "Oh good, then I don't have to write it again. Can I use the paper?" I reached out for it. "I want to make a treasure map for Marney."

"I will discuss this letter with your father when he gets home. For now, you need to go to your room and do your homework," she insisted, taking the paper, folding it and placing it into her apron.

"Already done," I lied.

"Let's see it then," she uttered, knowing full well the falsity of my statement.

I pointed to my head and said, "All up here."

"That's not done. Go to your room. Finish your homework and don't come out till it's done. If it's not done by dinner, there will be none."

Jane was sure angry.

Well, if I wanted to eat, then I had to get my homework done. But the truth of the matter was, I wasn't hungry. I smiled. I don't need dinner.

Journal Topic #42 If I could be invisible I would----

Dear Journal,

If I could be invisible I would ride on top of cars and make people wonder what's holding their hoods down. I would walk into airplanes and fly off to different places. If I could be invisible, I would sneak into the places who send those bills to Fred and Jane and I would delete our address from their files. Then I would walk into my favorite frozen yogurt shop and get the biggest cup of frozen yogurt with all the chocolate sprinkles I wanted and walk out while everyone in the place ran for their lives shouting, "Ghost!" That would be hilarious.

But most of all, sometimes I already feel invisible. I have no friends, except for the people who want to cheat off my tests at school and the entire dweeb table at lunch. I mean sure, they sit with me, I sit with them. But, they never say a word. No one talks to me. Not even the brainy nerds. Do I intimidate even them?

What's worse is the fact that I want to be invisible. I think life would be better if I was anonymous. Instead I'm this freak of nature, a tiny body with an adult thinking mind. I try to be invisible, especially in the bathroom. But to those girls, no one is out of their radar. Even if they pretend not to notice you, they notice you. They know you one way or another. They will know not to affiliate with you at all or they will know to tease you or they will know to get downright nasty crazy beyotch on you. Maybe I should erase that. But, I'm sure you've heard worse, Ms. Harper. So, I'll leave it in. What kind of a world would it be anyway, if I agreed with self-censorship?

Love,
Sam

11 FIRED

Marney came home early today. Yay!

But she wasn't happy. She was really mad. I heard her shouting. I know she wasn't shouting at Jane and Fred, but I was very surprised. I'd never heard her shouting before except when she played basketball and she was fervently trying to win. But that wasn't anger anyway, that was determinism at its best. No, she was mad. Something happened.

I heard Jane and Fred trying to soothe her and calm her down. I peeked out of my room to see what was happening. I heard little tidbits.

"'Watch what you say, Marney, they told me.'" She repeated.

I think she was having the same dilemma that I was having earlier today.

"'She's our best customer.'"

I was trying to work out the bits and pieces. A girl came into the shop and Marney had to treat her nicely, but she's on a rival team. Not really a rival team anymore. But, I can understand why Marney would be upset. It was the friend of the teammate who caused Marney's injury. I didn't think she cared much about that girl. I figured she knew it was an accident.

I walked into the kitchen and everyone went silent. I wasn't having that so I shouted, "What's happening?!!"

"Young Lady," Fred said, "why are you shouting?"

I looked at Fred. "I wanted to be part of the action. Everyone else is shouting."

It seemed logical enough to me. I think it seemed logical enough to Fred too because he kind of smiled and nodded his head. Jane was not amused. She never is. I thought she'd send me to my room again but that didn't happen. Instead Marney spoke up.

"Amy Chesterton, from Blackwood School, she came in today..."

I looked at her.

"She was with friends. I heard her tell them who I was."

I walked closer to Marney.

"Then she said, my accident was the best thing that happened to Blackwood because without me, my old team doesn't stand a chance."

My eyes started to tear. Marney's were already damp. I put my hand on her leg.

"I told her to shut the f---- up!"

Marney threw my hand off her leg.

"Don't touch me!" She wheeled herself around and headed toward her room. "Don't anyone touch me!"

I looked at Fred and Jane. Jane had her hands covering her mouth. Her eyes were wet too.

Fred looked at me, put his hand on my shoulder and said softly, "It's okay, Sam. She's just upset. She'll come around."

I was crying pretty hard now. Fred grabbed me and hugged me.

"Don't touch me, Fred." I wriggled out of his hug, cried and ran back to my room.

"Did she call me Dad?"

"No, she still called you Fred, Fred." Jane threw a kitchen towel at Fred and cried then walked out of the kitchen.

It's not his fault. Everyone seemed to be out of sorts today. That damned Amy. How dare she? I should write a letter!

I knocked on Marney's door. "Marney? It's me...Squirt." I knocked again, this time louder, in case she had headphones on.

"Ok, Squirt, you can come in. But, close the door behind you."

I was right. She was on the computer watching old videos. Why does she torture herself that way? I don't understand it. I try to, but I don't.

I hugged her. This time she didn't push me away. She hugged me harder. I missed this. This moment was really needed for both of us.

"What else happened, Marney?"

She looked at me and moved the hair out of my eyes, "They fired me."

Had I caused this? Did I make her get fired because I didn't want her to work? I told Jane I didn't want her to work. I wrote it in my journal. I hugged her harder.

"I'm sorry Marney. It's all my fault. I didn't mean it. I'm sorry."

She laughed. "All your fault?" She looked at me and smiled. "It's not your fault. You didn't do anything. Just because you were miserable and didn't want me to work, doesn't mean you did anything wrong."

"You knew about that?" I asked her.

"I would've been a fool not to know it." She rubbed my head. "We're best sisters, aren't we?"

She put her little pinky out and I put my little pinky out and we did the pinky shake.

"Come on, Squirt." Marney started to wheel toward her door.

"Where are we going, Marney?"

"Outside to shoot some hoops. Where else?"

This letter writing thing really works!

We went outside and started to play. Marney tossed the ball to me.

"Hey Marney, watch this!" I stood stiff as a board and threw the ball in the basket underhanded. It went in and I jumped for joy.

"Good job, Squirt." She put her hand up and we high-fived.

Journal Topic #18 I always feel good when----

Dear Journal,

I always feel good when Marney and I are getting along. Yay! We shot hoops till really late last night and the best part about it was, Fred and Jane didn't even come out to tell us to go to bed. They just let us play as long as we wanted.

I tried my best and threw the ball many times. It didn't matter to Marney how many times I threw it or that I hardly made a shot. She just kept coaching me and telling me to try again. She showed me how to put my arms and hands just right and even how to jump. I liked it. It was fun.

Love,
Sam

12 TRUE LOVE

Journal Topic #14 You can tell someone likes you by----

Dear Journal,

You can tell someone likes you by the way they look at you and if they follow you around a lot and want to hang out with you.

I'm sitting in English class and the teacher just introduced a new kid and he's not like any other boy. He's young and smart like me. Woohoo! Who knew there were more people out there like me? I'm so excited.

Since he doesn't know anyone, I think I will introduce myself. I heard he's some kind of chess champion, which makes him nerdy, but who cares? He's like me!

Love,
Sam

I introduced myself to the new boy in school. His name is Cong, it sounds like Kong, though. He's from China. Well, not really from China. His parents are Chinese. He speaks perfect English. He was born here. I talked to him at lunch. He sat with us Geeks. He said he was going to a Chinese school.

"But, my parents took me out. They called me a disappointment because I wasn't competing with my peers at the school."

"Here, you'll be a God," I told him. "So, how old are you?"

"I'm nine. How old are you?"

"I'm seven."

He didn't believe me for almost the whole day. But, he came around about 6th period in Biology. He doesn't like Biology. It's his least favorite subject. I kind of like it, though. Cells and stuff. It's like outer space is filled with planets and stars and our bodies have the same kind of thing going inside, only with cells and organs.

"What did you get on your IQ test?" Cong asked me.

"I don't know. I didn't ask," I replied.

Cong is all about numbers. That's his specialty. Numbers, strategy, that kind of intelligent thought.

"Mine is one hundred and forty." He sounded disappointed when he said it. Probably the same tone of disappointment his parents gave him when they found out.

"Oh, so you're only borderline genius," I teased.

He put his head down. Wow, he must have really been scolded. This score is really tormenting him. "Hey," I said, "we're ninety five percent smarter than any of these kids."

He smiled. I figured out how to cheer him up, just blow up his head a little. Now I had someone to be superior with and he was an older man, too. That was the best part about it.

"So, you want to be study buddies?" I asked.

"I'm not sure if I'm allowed to do that," he responded.

"Why not?"

"My parents are really strict."

"No harm in asking, right?" I said to him.

He looked dismayed but said, "I guess not."

The next day Cong came to school and he was more quiet and shy than the first day. I didn't get it. And plus, my new friend was avoiding me. How did that happen?

"Hey Cong!" I shouted to him as he walked past. "Hey!"

Some older kids were walking past too and they started shouting, "Yeah, hey King Kong. Where are you going? Your girlfriend wants you."

They all laughed at him and Cong kept walking, avoiding all of us. I gave the kids a dirty look and walked past them quickly to try to catch up with Cong.

"Hey Cong," I shouted as I finally caught up to him and held him back by his backpack. I didn't know I was that strong.

"What do you want?"

"What's the matter?" I asked.

"I'm not supposed to talk to you. I'm supposed to just keep my head down in the books. Not get overly noticed. Not get lured in by girls and especially not cute American girls."

"Did you just say I was cute?" I blushed.

Then he blushed too. He turned away from me and rushed off to class.

I was smiling from ear to ear. I had a boyfriend. I rushed to catch up with him again.

"You know, I can help you."

"What do you know? You're just a girl," he stated.

"One forty-four," I stated to him aggressively.

Cong stopped in his tracks. "What?"

"My I.Q.," I said, "it's one forty-four."

He went red again and then his shoulders slumped even further down. "Beaten by a girl," he said, "again."

"I didn't mean anything by it. Just, we can study together. Anything you're not great at, like Biology, I can help you and anything I'm not great at, you can help me."

So we made a pact right there never to make ourselves or each other feel smaller and to always help each other. Which meant, I had to do homework--every day--from now on.

"It's the only way my parents are going to let us be friends," he said to me.

And that's what convinced me. I actually was going to do homework. At least we could do homework together.

The next day, I told Marney I didn't need her to pick me up till later, that I was going to stay after school and do homework in the library.

"Do you have a fever?" She put her hand on my head, "Maybe I should take you to the E.R.," then she laughed.

"Stop it, Marney. I am serious."

She rubbed my head and made my hair stand on end. "Good for you, Squirt. It's about time."

I guess it was. Weird how I was doing it because of a boy. But, I guess I had more in common with the crazy girls of the bathroom than I thought. Who knew?

Before Marney got fired, she told me, there was a boy who came into the shop-a lot. You'd never think Marney could fall for anyone. Even I thought basketball was the only love in her life. But, no, this boy had come in and changed the way she viewed herself. He flirted with her the whole time he was there and both of his legs worked. He wasn't handicapped like she was. I didn't know she could like someone who had both legs working. But, I guess it was possible. She doesn't know if she'll see him again.

"It doesn't matter," Marney told me. "Maybe he flirts with all the girls, with legs or not."

"Hey, you've got legs. They just don't work." I responded happily.

Maybe that was the wrong tone to take because she suddenly looked less thrilled with her condition. "Oh, damn it," she said, "I'll never get out of this chair!"

I looked at her apologetically.

She wanted so much to have her old life back. "There are so many things I've never done!" she proclaimed.

"Like having a boyfriend?" It was an innocent question. But, it didn't help much. I needed a way to steer the conversation in a different direction. Something that could make her feel better. "Want me to make you a grilled cheese sandwich Marney?"

Marney looked at me. "Why not?"

She and I went to the kitchen and I turned on the TV and then pulled out the stuff to make her the sandwich. Marney's eyes were glued to the TV screen.

"Marney?"

Marney pointed to a Tide detergent commercial with her mouth wide open.

"What?" I asked. "It's laundry soap."

"That's him," Marney said. "That's the guy."

"The guy in the Tide commercial flirted with you?"

"Who flirted with who?" Fred walked in and we both looked at him like we were holding a She-Woman, Man-Hater Club meeting and he just walked into the middle of it.

"Oh! Uh, well, I guess I'll watch TV in the other room." He walked back out.

Marney and I burst into laughter.

"Do you think he lives around here, Marney?" I asked her.

She smiled. "He did come in a lot."

"I mean really what are the odds that he would just walk into our town, your yogurt store. He must live here."

"You may be right, Squirt." Marney said, "I gotta get my job back."

"What? Why?" I really didn't like that idea.

"You've got a boyfriend and you're seven. Why are you the only one who should be allowed to have happiness?"

She had a point. I was happy now that Cong was at my school. I had a friend, a smart friend and he was around my age. A plan formed in my head. "Okay Marney, I think I can help you."

The next day, I had to tell Cong I couldn't study after school. But, I promised him I would do my homework at home. He didn't believe me until I crossed my heart and hoped to die, stick a needle in my eye. He's so demanding.

When Marney picked me up from school, we went directly to the shop. There were some teenagers at the counter and I spoke up first, "We'd like to see the manager, please."

One of them went to the back and Marney's old manager came out. "What's going on Marney?" he asked her.

"Mr. Reiss, I'd like my job back," Marney stated surely.

Mr. Reiss looked displeased at being called out for this. "I don't think I can do that Marney. You know on account of what happened."

Marney looked more determined as ever. "I know what happened. But, do you know what happened? Do you really know, Mr. Reiss?"

"I don't know what you're talking about Marney. You know we just cannot have customers treated that way," he replied.

I butted in on that one. "Mr. Reiss, I'm Marney's sister, Samantha." I handed him a handwritten business card that I made myself in Art class that day. I wanted to be official. "I want you to know that if Marney doesn't get her job back, we will have no choice but to go to our friends at the paper and tell them all about the discrimination against handicapped here at your workplace and, of course, we'll also be speaking to a lawyer. Our father owns a business and because of that, we have access to the best lawyers in this county. Now, you can go ahead and think on that for a day or two, but don't wait too long and when you're ready to make a deal, then call me on that number."

Mr. Reiss was red as brick. "Who do you think you are, Young Lady?"

"I'm her manager," I retorted. "Feel free to call me any time this evening to discuss the details of her rehiring, but not too late because I have school in the morning."

Marney and I scooted towards the exit pretty fast. Weird how the universe works though. The moment we rolled out of the shop, Marney's crush was about to walk in. He looked right at Marney and gave her a huge smile.

"Are you off?" he asked her.

"Me?" she asked.

He nodded.

Marney stumbled to find the words, "Um, yeah, I mean, no, I am not sure if I will be working there anymore."

"Really? That's a shame. I only come in here to see you."

He certainly wasn't shy.

Marney blushed. I blushed too and I suddenly felt like a third wheel. "Marney, can we go home now?" I wanted to be cruising on her lap and on my way home.

"Can I walk you home?" The pretty boy smiled at her. Did his teeth sparkle? Wow, I think they did.

Marney could not resist. "Sure, yeah, ok." Marney would've said yes another five different ways if I hadn't have stopped her.

"It's three miles!" I shouted to him.

"No problem. I work out three hours every day," he boasted.

"I bet you do," Marney said out loud. Oh man. She's worse than the girls in the bathroom. He smiled and started to grab the back of her wheelchair.

"Uh, oh!" I said as I cleared my throat in warning.

"Oh, no, don't do that, please," Marney quickly rolled out of his grip. I may be handicapped but I'm not disabled. I do this every day and I won't have someone push me like an old woman."

"My bad," he said. What a stupid phrase. Who on this green earth came up with it--my bad--geez!

A few miles and a few flirtations later, the two blushing exercise addicts and I reached home. Marney looked at him, "You know how to get back from here?"

He looked around. "Not really."

I bet he knew.

"Do you want to come inside? I'm sure we can google it." Marney said.

I happened to see an iphone tucked in his pocket, but all the same, he came in.

"Wait, wait..." I stopped him. "We don't even know your name. You spent all this time flirting with my sister and do you even know hers?"

"Yeah, it's Marney and you're Sam," he boldly stated.

Damn! "Oh yeah? And who are you?"

"I'm Zack," he said, "Zack Winterberry."

I looked at Marney, "Winterberry?" I kind of mouthed the words, "Marney Winterberry?"

Marney sneered at me and mouthed, "Stop."

I let Zack pass and we went into the house. Jane and Fred had beaten us home. I didn't realize how long it took us to walk. Maybe it was because the lovebirds gazed too much into each other's eyes and less on the road.

At least this meant she wouldn't go back to the job.

Jane saw us first, "Who's your guest, Marney?"

"This is Zack."

"Zack Winterberry," he said stretching out his hand to Jane.

Fred walked in at that moment and did the most embarrassing, "Is that the guy?" whisper to Marney and me.

Marney mouthed the words, "Dad, please," while I nodded in agreement to Fred's question.

"I'm Jane, this is my husband, Fred."

Zack shook Fred's hand too. "Nice to meet you, Sir. You have a very nice home."

This is the same guy who said "My bad." He sure is a good actor.

"So, do you go to school with Marney?" Jane was pretty suspicious of everyone.

"No ma'am. I'm out of school. I'm working," Zack responded.

"Oh, working already?" Jane asked. "Where about?"

"All over really," Zack said, "I'm an actor."

"An actor," Jane responded, "how nice." She didn't sound genuine. Jane thinks actors are all poor or on drugs. "Marney can I speak to you alone in the other room?" She guided Marney out.

"So, have I seen you in anything?" Fred asked.

Zack huffed his chest and straightened his back. "Well, sir, if you turn on the TV, I've got three commercials running at the same time and I'm about to start a TV pilot."

"That's something." Fred responded. "Well done, Son. Keep up the good work."

Marney and Jane came back into the room. Jane looked like Marney had just sent her through the ringer. Jane said, "Zack, you must stay for dinner and tell us all about this pilot."

"Oh you overheard that, well, I should get back and-"

"Nonsense, Fred will drive you home after dinner. Won't you, Fred?" Jane pushed.

"Sure. Not a problem." Fred said.

Marney smiled.

I looked at Marney's lovesick eyes. "Oh brother." I said. I've done it again.

13 THE LAW OF GRAVITY

Journal Topic #20 At night I like to----

Dear Journal,

At night I like to pretend there is no such thing as gravity and I can float off wherever I want. There is so much more world to see. I would visit the stars and maybe even Mars. I like to imagine myself free of the laws of gravity and even in my dreams, I can fly. When I do that, I can control every motion with my mind. I don't have to flap my arms like a bird. I just think if I want to go down or up and when I'm landing, I just put my legs down and I can land and be stable on my own two legs again. But, the flying part, that's really the best.

Love,
Sam

Today's the day. Marney said she would go with me to that Health Expo where the doctor is speaking about conditions like Marney's. I hope she doesn't back out of it. Fred is taking us and everything. It will be good to look into these new techniques.

"No. I'm not going," Marney said as she threw a small basketball into a hoop on her wall.

"But, you promised," I retorted. "I arranged everything. Fred's going to drive us there. Everything is arranged. You promised." I looked at her with angry eyes.

"Why do you want this so bad, Sam?" she asked.

"Why don't you?" I answered, a little beaten.

Fred knocked on Marney's door. "Ready, Ladies?"

"No," Marney answered.

"Not yet," I said. "Marney, give it a chance. Good things are happening. You wanted to meet Zack and poof, like magic, you met him. Sure you had to get suspended from school and then fired first, but something good came out of that."

Marney started to see reason, I think. She didn't protest right away. "But, Squirt, you don't understand. I've looked at all this before and it's been nothing but disappointment. I don't want you to get your hopes up."

"Maybe that's the problem, Marney," I replied, "maybe we have too little hope."

Another knocking sounded at the bedroom door. "Just a minute!" Marney and I both shouted in unison.

"Oh, yeah, sorry." That was the voice of Zack.

Marney and I looked at each other and went to the door. Marney opened it. "Zack?" She looked out.

I peeked around the corner and then ran into the living room. Zack was seated on the couch and as Marney rolled in, he stood up. "Hi," he said.

"What are you doing here?" Marney asked.

"I just thought I'd drop by and see how you were. Your dad says you're going to that health expo."

"Yeah, we are, so we don't really have time to chat," I said to him.

"Sam!" Marney shouted.

"What?" I replied.

Zack jumped in, "I'm going too. When your dad said you were going, I thought it would be cool. Maybe we could all ride together or...I'd be happy to take you."

"In what?" Marney asked.

"In my truck," he replied, "it's just outside." He pointed out the front door.

"Oh really?" I said, "I thought it was in the kitchen."

Marney was not happy with my sarcasm. But, on the plus side, it did mean that she was going and that she'd keep her promise. Zack saves the day, again. Yee-haw.

The Health Expo was humongous! There was every kind of green gobby food and drink on the planet and maybe a few from Mars, too. We walked around for what seemed like hours in this endless maze of booths and health nuts, doctors, chiropractors, acupuncturists, physical therapists, magnet people, crystal people, gurus of every shape and kind. I felt like I had just walked into an episode of Star Trek Deep Space 9. Maybe I was hallucinating after drinking that bottle of Kombucha. They said it was tea, but I swear my legs got loopy.

Finally, it was time for the doctor's talk on Spinal Injuries. We all walked over to the section where that event was being held. I was surprised that there weren't too many people there. We rolled up to the front of the room. Zack moved a chair away so Marney could put her wheelchair there. I sat next to Marney and Zack sat to my right.

The doctor's speech was interesting, but even with my level of smarts, I still didn't get it all. I still had a lot of questions and the doctor was very willing to answer them. He even took Marney, Zack and me to a little booth he had set up nearby and showed us something really really cool.

"Marney," the doctor said, "today, I want to give you something special for coming to hear me speak." He picked up what looked like a bicycle helmet.

"She doesn't need a bicycle helmet, Doctor," I said.

He laughed. "It's not a bicycle helmet. It's the latest in virtual reality technology and I use it for my paraplegics and paralyzed patients. It's not a cure. It's just an opportunity to feel your legs again."

"Feel my legs?" Marney asked excitedly.

The doctor smiled. I looked at Marney. Marney looked at Zack who smiled back at her and gestured for her to go try it.

"Do it," I said.

Marney rolled over to the machine and the doctor placed the helmet on her head. It fit over her eyes and everything--built in glasses, too.

The doctor turned the machine on and suddenly I saw Marney's whole body jump a little.

"Her legs moved!" I shouted.

The doctor responded, "Perhaps, but this is not medicine. It's not even physical therapy. This is mental therapy. Getting her body to relax and let go of the idea of the injury."

"Can she hear us? Maybe we shouldn't discuss this around her. Wouldn't it confuse the illusion?" Zack asked.

"No, she can't hear us. It's not a problem. Inside that helmet is a whole new world. She's walking, she's swimming, jumping, whatever she wants. It has all the senses, sights, smells, sounds of the world outside, except she can walk."

"She can feel like she's walking?" I asked.

"Yes, she can feel everything," the doctor replied.

"So, it's any world she wants?" I asked.

"What do you mean?" the doctor asked.

"Can she be floating in space?" I asked.

"She sure can. If she wants to, she can even float in space."

"Wow! Me next!" I shouted.

"Well, Young Lady, it's not a toy. This is used strictly for my patients. I brought it today to introduce it to possible new patients."

The doctor seemed to be getting annoyed with me. I wondered why.

"Are your parents with you?" He looked at me, smiled and then looked around the room expecting me to point someone out to him.

"Nope. Just us." I looked around and Zack was gone.

The doctor turned off the machine and removed the helmet from Marney's head. Marney had tears in her eyes and a big smile on her face.

The doctor looked at Marney, "Are you ok?"

Marney looked at him and smiled, "Thank you."

"You're welcome, Young Lady." He handed her a business card and said, "Please give this card to your parents. Here's a brochure too and feel free to drop by my office so we can discuss the new treatments and advancements in surgery, in more detail. I would like the opportunity to review your case, if you want me to."

Marney looked like she'd just seen an angel. I was happy that she was happy.

"Where's Zack?" she asked.

"I don't know. He was here a minute ago." I stated. "Want me to go find him?" I started to walk away.

"Hey, hey, don't wander off without me," she said. "We probably shouldn't go too far away from the booth. He'll probably have an easier time of finding us if we stay put."

I smirked. "But, for how long? I don't want to just stand there. There's all sorts of wacky stuff to look at and try."

Like I said, I like biology and this convention center looked like a great big biology experiment. It was pretty cool.

"Oh! Look at that, Marney!"

I ran off to look at a great big blow up monkey doll inside of a monkey space ship.

Marney rolled quickly after me, "I told you not to run off!"

The people at this booth are what you call animal rights activists. I'm not sure what they meant with the blow up monkey doll inside the spaceship, but they had all sorts of nasty videos playing showing sick animals. "Little girl," one of them called to me, "do you eat meat?"

"Yes," I told him.

"Well, meet your meat!" he called as he pulled out what seemed to be a dead chicken with its feathers gone and big lumps on it.

I shrunk back in disgust. Marney pulled me away from the booth, "Come on, let's get out of here and find Zack."

We didn't need to look much further because there he was, just a couple of tables down selling some kind of diet drink, swarmed by a group of pretty girls. He was autographing the sample cups he gave them. Some actor! We went up to him.

"What are you doing?" Marney asked him.

Zack shooed away the last girl with a drink and a smile. He turned to Marney, "I am the official spokesperson for this diet drink. I sell it on TV and my contract says I have to be here at the Health Expo for a couple hours. Giving autographs, samples, you know..."

Marney didn't seem too happy about that but I could tell she wasn't going to get mad. I started to pull on her arm to tug her away. "It's okay, Marney, it can be just you and me now. We can explore for a while."

"Okay, Squirt, let's go." Marney looked at Zack, "We'll be back in an hour or so."

Zack saluted her and then turned to greet the long line of cute girls waiting to talk to him and get his autograph. The giggling seemed to give Marney the same reaction that nails would have on a chalkboard.

Other cool things we visited were booths with signs that stated, "See a thought," and "Food Games," and then there was, "Watch your blood in action!" Marney got queasy at that last booth. Funny, you would think that she wouldn't mind a little bloodshed. I mean, okay, basketball is not exactly a bloodsport, but there were plenty of scrapes and cuts before the big injury.

We were about to go back to Zack's booth when I suddenly felt the urge to use the bathroom and I was desperate. I looked about the great hall and I saw no signs for the bathroom. Marney and I went along a little while and I finally just asked someone where it was. The lady pointed the way and I told Marney, "I'm sorry Marney, but I have to run," and I did.

I could hear Marney call out to me as she rolled herself to try and keep up. But, I needed to get there fast, there was no way I was going to have an accident and then get driven home in wet pants by a guy who is on TV.

When I came out of the bathroom, Marney was waiting for me outside. She was pretty mad that I didn't wait for her. But then Zack showed up and he smiled at her, and she seemed to forget all about me running off. He walked with us to the car, helped Marney inside after me and then drove us home.

Fred was watering the lawn outside when we pulled up. He walked over the passenger door and waved, hose in hand. I waved back. Marney smiled. Zack took the wheelchair out of the back and set it up. Fred opened the door and put Marney in the wheelchair. I hopped out of the truck and ran up to the house.

"Don't you have something to say, Young Lady?" Fred called to me.

"Thanks Zack!" I yelled back and ran inside. I wanted to get inside as fast as possible to go online and check out this doctor's website. After seeing everything I saw at the Health Expo, I was thinking really positive that something could be done for Marney.

14 BACK TO SCHOOL

Marney's two-week suspension from school seemed to fly by. Lucky for her, too, because she has a hard time being away from friends, especially those from her team. She went back as cheerful as ever.

I, on the other hand, would be glad to be away from school for two weeks. Because during this time, I felt especially vulnerable. My usual sassy front was a little jarred out of whack because Cong had put up a wall of his own recently. I think it had to do more with his parents than with me. But, I had to figure out how to fix whatever was broken. With boys, that is hard because they don't talk much.

In English class, I asked Cong, "We're still study-buddies, right?"

He just responded with a sort of questionable grunt.

"I did my homework," I told him. "Come on, don't make me beg to be friends. Because I won't."

Plus, I had the added benefit of being watched, wherever I went, by the bathroom girls, so much that, I ceased going to the bathroom at school altogether and waiting to pee until I got home got to be a real annoying sport.

"Let me in, I gotta go in, quick!" I ran away from Marney pretty darn quick and practically slammed through the front door of the house and then made a mad dash for the bathroom. Ahh... This really has got to stop.

"You've been doing that a lot, lately," Marney remarked. "Is there something wrong?"

"No, no," I replied, "I just forgot to go."

"You forgot to go?"

"Yeah, quit nagging me about it, Marney."

"Okay," she responded with a sigh.

I wasn't going to allow her to get into trouble again. I had to stand up on my own two feet, at some point anyway.

I changed the subject. "Now that your suspension is over, can you play on the team again, Marney?"

"Coach said my school suspension may be over but my game suspension is not," Marney revealed. She had tears in her eyes. "We've got a really big game coming up. I don't want to miss it. I even told Zack about it. He thinks I'm gonna play."

"Uh oh," I said. "Can't you just tell him you spoke too soon?"

"No, damn it. I want to play." Marney threw her basketball into the little basket on her wall. She always does that when she's thinking.

"What are you thinking about doing, Marney?" I asked.

"I don't know. I gotta prove to the coach that he needs me back on the team." She kept throwing the ball into the little hoop on her wall.

15 A DANCE TO REMEMBER

D inner!" we heard Jane call out.

Marney and I left her room and planted ourselves beside Fred at the kitchen table. Jane served dinner and Fred turned on the TV to watch the sports news.

"Fred? Can we just sit down without the TV on and have conversations like normal families do?" Jane asked.

"Normal families?" Marney asked with a laugh. "When has this family ever been normal?" Marney giggled and it made me giggle. Then Fred laughed, Jane smiled.

"Ok, can we sit down, eat and talk like extraordinary families?"

Fred leaned over and kissed Jane, "That's more like it."

Jane smiled. "Marney, I heard there is a dance going on at your school this weekend. I suppose Zack is taking you?"

I looked at Marney, "You didn't say anything to me, Marney."

Marney looked at me, "How would Zack know about the dance? And no, I'm not going. No one has asked me and when have I ever gone to a dance?"

Jane was a bit flustered but she collected herself, served some more food and answered, "I got a call from Zack today saying he was going to drop by and ask you."

I looked at Marney, "A little creepy, asking Jane's permission."

"I thought it was a sweet gesture. Lord knows we could do with some good old fashioned manners around here."

"When did you start praying?" Marney said to Jane.

"Oh boy," I exclaimed. I started to pull my plate of food close to me.

"Marney Alise Ferguson!" Jane exclaimed.

"Fred, can I eat in my room?"

"No you may not," Jane said to me. "Everyone stay seated and finish eating. We are going to have some uninterrupted, pleasant family time for once."

"Honey," Fred asked Jane, "can I just check the score of the..."

"No, you may not." Fred shut up pretty fast and we all sat there eating in silence.

It was kind of strange, but at the same time, it was also kind of peaceful. We'd never had a moment of silence over dinner, let alone ten minutes of silence. I realized, though, someone was going to have to bring the table back together in peace. I cleared my throat to say something when the doorbell rung--saved by the bell.

Fred put his napkin down, stood up and said, "I'll get it." He was pretty light on his feet. I heard him at the door. "Hello Zack," he said, "nice to see you again."

"Is Marney home?" Zack asked.

"Yes, let me get her," Fred responded.

Fred came into the kitchen. "Marney, you have a visitor."

Marney wheeled herself from the table, which was still silent, by the way, and became even more silent as we listened to know what was happening in the other room.

"Hi Marney," Zack said. "How have you been?"

"All right, I guess," she said.

"I came by to ask if I could be your date to your school's dance this Friday."

"How'd you know about it anyway?" Marney asked him.

"Well, I dropped by the school this afternoon to see if I could pick you up and take you home, but you weren't there. A student handed me this flier."

There was some silence then. And we all leaned our heads a little closer to the door as if our heads were magnetized.

Finally Marney spoke up. "How do you think I'm supposed to go to a dance, Zack?"

"If you can play basketball, you can dance."

Then we didn't hear anything else except for the door closing. When Marney arrived back into the kitchen, we all looked at her. She was holding a bright green flier.

"Looks like I'm going to the dance with Zack on Friday." She smiled a little unsure smile and shrugged her shoulders, but still I could see that gleam in her eye.

"That's great, Sweetheart," Jane said and hugged her.

"Way to go, Sport," Fred said as he punched Marney's arm.

Journal Topic #22 I would like to learn to ----

Dear Journal,

I would like to learn to dance. Maybe it sounds dumb, but I've never been invited to a dance and I think, if I were invited, I'd like to know how to dance. I'd like to be the underdog, the one that nobody expects to win, and I'd like to dance like Michael Jackson. I think I could really rise up in popularity if I knew how to dance. I wonder if our school has dances. If they do, I wonder if Cong would ask me to go.

Don't tell Cong, but, I think I would really like that.

Love,
Sam

The night of the dance was a bit awkward for Marney. She hadn't been in a dress since she was about fourteen and was asked by this giant Albino named, Barry White, to the "Make it Last Forever" dance. I know it sounds like I'm making it up. But, I'm not. It's in Marney's 9th grade yearbook. He was, of course, a basketball player, but he still seemed to tower over the rest of the team.

Jane helped Marney get dressed. They told me I was getting in the way so I was sent out of the room. I could hear them struggling, though. Jane would tell Marney, "Stop fidgeting."

Marney would tell Jane, "Relax."

I guess it was hard on both of them. You gotta hand it to Jane, though, it's over a hundred pounds she's got to lift and it's not like she gets any practice in the construction company as a receptionist. The only thing she lifts there is a pen.

She used to have to help Marney wash and dress and everything until Marney relearned those things on her own. It's only tonight that they seem to be having so much trouble. "For crying out loud, Marney, let me do it!" I heard Jane yell.

"I can zip it up now. I got it!" Marney yelled back.

Fred walked by me as I eavesdropped at Marney's door.

"What's happening, Sam?" Fred asked.

"Girl stuff," I replied.

"Girl stuff," he confirmed, "got it." Then he walked away. I heard the TV switch on to the Sports channel.

Finally, the door to Marney's room opened and Jane and Marney came out. Marney looked beautiful. She had her hair all done up and she wore makeup. I don't know if I've ever seen her in makeup and the dress looked beautiful on her. It even hid the chair a little.

"You look beautiful, Marney." I said to her.

"Thanks, Squirt." She smiled.

The doorbell rang. Fred answered and Zack stood at the door in a tuxedo. He looked much better than the boys at my school.

"Wow!" I said. Suddenly, I felt guilty. Maybe I should call Cong.

Marney stood beside me, mouth wide open. Zack smiled and suddenly, she recognized it was a little obvious. She closed her mouth and swallowed a little shyly.

"You look beautiful, Marney," Zack said. "You ready?"

Marney pulled herself together, toughened up, straightened her back and said, "Yep." Then she wheeled herself out the door, down the ramp and toward Zack's truck. She looked back at Fred. "Don't wait up!"

Fred walked to the patio, "Yeah, right," he said skeptically. "Have her home by midnight Zack."

"Yes, Sir," Zack said.

"I mean it," Fred reiterated, "Midnight. That's my first born."

"Okay, Dad. Close the door," Marney called out.

Jane pulled Fred inside the house, looked at Marney and waved then went inside and shut the door while I stood at the window and watched them leave.

It was getting late when Marney came back home. I was in bed, but I wasn't sleeping. I really wanted to stay up and wait for Marney to come back and tell me about her fairy tale dance. But, that didn't happen. Instead, I heard shouting. I jumped up and ran to my door to listen.

She came in through the front door and slammed it in a fit.

"Buzz off, Zack!" I heard her shout.

I know she didn't say "buzz" but, I'm not supposed to say those words even though they've been part of my vocabulary since starting the 7th grade. Jane and Fred were trying to find out what happened to Marney. Fred was really angry even though he didn't know what happened yet.

"Did he hurt you? Did he try to touch you?" Fred asked.

"Jesus, Dad, I'm not eight."

"Marney, please, just tell us what happened," Jane demanded.

Marney looked at her watch. "Just turn on the news."

"What?" Fred asked.

"What for, honey?" Jane repeated.

"Just do it. It's probably on the ten o'clock news right now. Just turn it on."

Fred switched on the television in the living room and surfed through all the news channels. "What are you trying to show us, Marney?"

"There!" she shouted, "Right there!"

Fred stopped switching the channels. A news reporter was on the television talking to kids at Marney's school dance. He then turned to Marney and Zack. "This is it," Marney said.

"Oh my God, you're on TV!" I shouted as I ran out of my room and stood next to them by the TV. They didn't even notice me.

"We're live from St. Augustine's High School in Cherry Hill, and who did we just run into? Actor, Zack Winterberry and his date..."

Zack spoke into the reporter's microphone, "Marney. She's the school's handicapped basketball star."

Marney seemed stunned.

The reporter continued asking Zack questions about how he decided to take Marney to the dance.

"Why is this news?" Jane asked.

"It's not," Marney answered. "It's a creepy paparazzi show that finds and follows stars."

"How did he find Zack?" I chimed in. Everyone looked at me like I shouldn't be there. But I didn't budge. I just looked at Marney.

"They didn't have to find him. He told them where he was going to be and when and who with."

"I'm not following, Sweetheart, and this is bad because?" Fred asked.

"Don't you see, Dad?" Marney responded. "He set me up. This was all for publicity. It was so he could look good and sweet and kind to his fans. He's building his publicity for the new show he's starring in. He never really liked me. All I am to him is a publicity stunt. He pities me." She broke down into tears and rolled away to her room.

"Bastard!" I said.

"Samantha, go to your room!" Jane and Fred demanded simultaneously.

I walked off sluggishly.

"March!" Jane called.

I hustled to my room and shut myself in, but I listened against the wall to hear if Marney was all right. She was still crying.

16 INSTANT REPLAY

After Marney's dreadful date, I realized I hadn't done what I said I was going to do. So, I set out to make it happen. I pulled out all the brochures I collected from the Health Expo and started to comb through them. So many therapies available for so many ailments. Water therapy, magnet therapy...I looked through them all until I finally found it. Doctor Wade Mackey, Virtual Reality Therapy.

I was going to call Doctor Wade Mackey and get Marney to go into his office for another virtual reality treatment. She had such a great experience last time and the doctor did say they were making some advancements in surgical procedures, too. My plan was fool proof. I just needed to get Fred to agree to it.

In the morning, before school, I put the brochure on Fred's desk where he was sure to see it. I even put the business card and flier from the expo on his chair so when he sat down, he was certain not to miss it, even if he did switch on the TV.

Then I made breakfast. I boiled eggs. I burnt toast. I even poured all the orange juice into glasses and set the table. Fred came in and then Jane. They were shocked. Fred sat down at his chair, "Did you do this?"

I nodded with a smile.

He wiggled a little and pulled the flier out from his seat and set it on the table.

"Want some coffee?"

Jane sat down too, and broke into a soft hard boiled egg. The yellow oozed out all over her plate.

"Woops, sorry Jane, too soft."

"That's ok, I'll just have it on the toast," she said, as she took the charred bread, buttered it and wiped it into the yellowy mess like there was nothing wrong with it.

"This is really a nice surprise, Sam," Fred said. "We should get Marney up."

"No, no!" I shouted. "Not yet. Not until you've eaten and read the paper." I gave him back the flier that he'd set aside and pointed to it. "Look at this, Fred. It looks good, doesn't it?" I handed him the brochure. "And this."

"What is it?" Jane asked.

"It's this really cool helmet that you put on and you can fly. Marney tried it at the Health Expo and she could feel her legs!" I said enthusiastically.

But Fred was skeptical. I could hear it in his tone of voice. "It says here, it's still in test phases, Samantha."

"But, he said, we could call him and make an appointment. I just want her to have that feeling again."

Marney rolled into the kitchen. Everyone went silent. "Okay, I know you've just been talking about me. Next time don't make it so obvious. What have they been saying, Squirt?"

I grabbed the brochure and held it up for Marney to see. "Remember this guy?" I asked. "Remember that machine? How you were walking?"

Marney grabbed the brochure. "Yeah, so what? It's just a game, it's not real life," Marney replied.

"If it feels real, it is real," I said. "You felt something, Marney. I know it."

"You should do it," Jane said.

We all looked at her.

"I've always thought, this is so hard. Why me? But, it didn't happen to me, Marney. It happened to my little girl and I'm not going to pretend that I don't hear you crying at night and that you don't miss your legs."

"Mom, but the cost," Marney said.

"I don't care." Jane hugged Marney. "Yes, we've got bills piling up. Yes, your father and I fight about it. But it's not your fault. It's no one's fault and we can handle it. We always have and we always will."

"It's that girl from the other team's fault!" I spoke up.

Marney stopped me. "It was an accident, that's all."

Fred smiled at Jane and then spoke up, "Your mom is right. After your accident, we should've kept looking. We gave up because we got overwhelmed and we thought you started to accept it and so we accepted it. But no, you don't have to accept it, anymore."

Fred got up and hugged Marney and Jane.

I couldn't resist. I walked over and hugged them too. "Group hug," I shouted. Everybody giggled.

Afterward, Fred called the doctor and set an appointment for Marney that week. She would do the virtual reality therapy again and then she'd be put through some tests to see if she was a candidate for a new surgery.

Everyone was so excited that no one could hardly do anything without thinking of Marney's possible recovery. I think it got mentioned once in every conversation we had for the rest of the week.

Finally, it was time to go to the doctor's office. Marney was really nervous. She wasn't excited anymore and she even cried a little. "Dad, I can't do this," she claimed. "I'm not ready for another letdown."

"Marney," Fred said, "we're all on your team here. No one is going to let you down. We'll be by your side cheering you on. But, you need to do this. The doctor said you have a real shot at overcoming this thing and I believe him."

We arrived at the doctor's office early. Fred always liked to be early to inspect everything at every job, before and after. So, when we got to the doctor's office Fred paced the office, measured it with his eyes, evaluated their molding and paint job and checked the desk with his level, which he always kept in his back pocket. The receptionist looked at him with a questioning glance.

"Sorry, force of habit. We're the Fergusons. Marney has an appointment to see Dr. Mackey."

The receptionist handed Fred some paperwork, "Fill this out and sign the bottom. The doctor is stuck in traffic and will be a little late. So, I'll get you started as soon as you're done with that."

Fred filled out the paperwork, occasionally asking Marney a question about the extent of her lack of feeling in her legs. Marney was getting anxious. "I don't feel anything, Dad. So, just put that."

"Okay, Marney." He wrote down what she said, signed the paperwork and gave it back to the receptionist.

The receptionist made a file for Marney and then said, "Marney, why don't you come on back and I'll get you set up."

Jane butted in, "Are you a doctor?"

"I'm a Nurse Practitioner. The regular receptionist is out on maternity leave."

"I see," Jane replied.

"Can I come, Marney?" Marney looked at me and nodded.

Marney rolled herself into the back office where the nurse took her temperature, blood pressure and a blood sample off her finger. "Ouch!" Marney said, "You could've warned me that you were gonna do that."

"I've been doing this job a long time and if I'd have warned you, it would've hurt more," she replied.

I laughed because I thought it might be true.

"Okay," the nurse said, "we're done here. Now I'll bring your parents in and show you all the machine and set you up with it."

The nurse walked out and asked Jane and Fred to step inside. They walked down the hall to a great big room with a screen, a game module, and a helmet. It looked like we were inside a big spacey game room. There were a few of them set up. The difference between these machines and the one at the health expo was the great big screen.

"What's the screen for?" I asked the nurse.

"It's so that we can see what Marney sees."

"Wow!" I replied.

"I'm going to hook you up, Marney. It's going to be slightly different than the machine at the expo. That was our older model. We don't allow the newer ones to leave the building. There are a few more bells and whistles to this one but with that, it means, there are more wires and hookups." She pulled out a sticky circle with a wire on it and she gave it to Marney. "Put this right over your heart."

Marney looked a little worried. "This isn't gonna shock me or anything, is it?"

"No dear, no," the nurse replied, "it's just a monitor. We want to monitor your heart and breathing while you're in the virtual reality treatment helmet."

"Okay, I guess." She stuck it under her shirt onto her chest. The nurse gave her another one for her lungs and told her where to put it. Then, she slid her wheelchair into a locking position with clamps on the floor. She gave Marney the helmet and Marney put it on.

The nurse picked up a microphone near one of the machines and switched it on. "Marney won't be able to hear us except if we speak through this microphone."

I ran up to the microphone, "Hi Marney," I shouted.

Marney said, "Hi Squirt. I'm ok."

The nurse looked at me sternly as if to say, I won't allow you to do that again. So I smiled shyly and tried to manage a blush. She bought it and let her scowl go.

"Marney, did you have anything in mind that you would like to try?" the nurse talked into the microphone.

"What do you mean?" Marney asked.

"You can do anything in this. It's like controlling your own dream. If you want to swim, you can swim or surf, ski, fly, play games. We can create it all."

"Can you be in deep space?" I shouted.

"Yes, you can even be in deep space," she replied.

"Basketball?" Marney asked from inside her virtual reality shell. "Can I play basketball?"

The nurse started pushing buttons on her console and replied, "Coming right up."

The screen outside Marney's head lit up with a thundering applause. There were screaming fans inside a great big arena with signs and banners and hot dog vendors, everything the mind could imagine. It was all there. And there was Marney. I couldn't see her face. But, I could see her legs. It was like we were watching everything from her point of view.

The referee started the ball toss to see who gets it. Marney was so fast, she practically flew to get that ball. I glanced over at Marney in real life and I could see her chair moving slightly back and forth as she controlled the game on the screen and in her head.

The crowd went wild when Marney grabbed that ball. She ran down the court like it was nobody's business and she slam-dunked that ball. The crowd went wild over and over again. With every shot, every block, every pass, I could hear Marney laugh. The crowds excited her and made her move even faster, go for even more shots. I looked over at Marney inside her helmet and I could tell she was getting tired. She was breathing hard and even though it was only a virtual game, she was really playing it.

When the doctor finally arrived and asked the nurse how long the machine was on, the nurse responded, "About thirty minutes."

The doctor began to shut down the machine and as he did, he talked to Marney through the microphone, "Marney, I'm going to turn the machine off now. You need to come back to us."

At that moment there was a whole lot of confusion, because Marney's legs on the screen tumbled to the floor like spaghetti. Her virtual reality legs weren't working. "There's something wrong," the doctor said. "That shouldn't happen."

"What do you mean, Doctor? What happened?" Fred asked.

"She shouldn't have been allowed to be in there for longer than fifteen minutes. The longer she's inside, the more wrapped up she is in that reality." He continued to shut the game down until everything had powered off. But Marney wasn't moving. Her body slumped in her chair.

Fred and Jane both gasped and ran toward Marney in the machine. The doctor removed the helmet and checked her vital signs. "She's fine. She's just in shock."

"What do you mean, in shock?" Jane asked angrily.

"It's almost as if she's relived her accident," the doctor replied.

"That can't be good," I said.

"No, quite the contrary. It can be good. Her vital signs are normal. Right now, she's in a small state of sleep as her body and mind figure out what happened and adjust to what she remembers."

"Will she be asleep long?" I asked.

"No, just another moment or two, I think," the doctor said.

"You think?" Fred demanded. "Doctor, we knew this was experimental but, if your machine put our daughter into a coma-"

"I'm not in a coma," Marney spoke up. "I'm okay," she told him. "I feel very strange, though. A little light-headed."

"That's just the side effects of the machine wearing off, Marney, nothing to be worried about."

I ran over to Marney, "Did you feel your legs again, Marney?"

She smiled at me and gave me a noogie, "Yeah, Squirt, I did. And it was really cool."

I smiled back while rubbing my head.

"What do we do next?" Marney asked the doctor.

Part Three – The Law of Have & Have Not

17 SURGERY AND TREATMENT COSTS MONEY

Apparently everything has a price. We all got so excited at the doctor's office we seemed to forget that doctor's offices run on power, staff and man hours and those cost money. It's not something you can just win like a prize. Everyone has to live and living costs money.

Once Fred and Jane sat down with the doctor to talk treatment plans, plus surgery and recovery time in the hospital, which would be billed separately, it came down to a decision. Fred and Jane had put away some money for Marney's college fund. There was no possible way to fund both. Marney would have to make a choice. Either the surgery, which could possibly fail, or the University. They reasoned that if she chose surgery, she could still go to a city college, but it's not likely they'd have wheelchair basketball.

Plus, there would be several more virtual reality treatments before the surgery was even performed. That was supposed to get her mind and body ready for the surgery and impending possibility that upon recovery, she could get up and walk almost perfectly. She would, of course, have some physical therapy but its intensity would be based upon what already was or wasn't accomplished.

"Marney, this is your decision," Fred said to her.

Doctor Mackey looked intensely at Marney. "You don't have to decide right now. Go home. Sleep on it for a few days. I will be here."

"Marney, honey," Jane said, "we will support whatever decision you make."

Marney looked at me. I hugged her. Then she opened up and said, "I'm a little tired."

"Ok, let's go home," Fred said. He stood up and offered his hand to the doctor. "Thank you, we'll get back to you."

"You're very welcome," Doctor Mackey responded.

Jane shook his hand, too. I held my hand out and he took it and I shook his hand. "Thanks," I said.

When we left the office everyone was silent. I thought Marney would be excited and that we'd all be smiling on the way home, just knowing everything was going to be all right. But instead, I felt bad. Marney was confused. Jane and Fred were a little worried, I think. It's like the new possibility threw a wrench into Marney's machine...everything she knew, everything she did, the way she worked, it all stopped. She had to rethink where she wanted to go in life and it was all because of me. I felt really bad.

Journal Topic #12 If I had a million dollars, I would----

Dear Journal,

If I had a million dollars, I would give it to my sister, Marney. She wouldn't have to choose between going to the University and having a surgery that could give her back her legs and she wouldn't have to give the money back. It would be for keeps.

I'm not old enough to play the lottery, but I have 13 dollars and 75 cents in my piggy bank. It would give Marney thirteen chances to win. Fourteen if she's got another quarter. A million dollars could be just six numbers away.

I could have a million dollars...

Love,
Sam

"Hey Marney," I went into her room with my giant pink piggy bank. It even has wings on it, symbolizing pigs flying. Because all dreams are possible. I like that piggy bank. It's not one of those ones you break either. You can just open it's belly to get out the money. So, I handed it to Marney.

"What's this for?" She asked.

"It's thirteen dollars and seventy five cents," I said to her. "You can use it to play the lottery. There's two million, five hundred thousand and seventy two dollars up for grabs. And if you have another quarter on you, then you have fourteen chances to win."

Marney laughed but there were also tears in her eyes. She put the piggy bank to the side, held her arms out to me and we hugged. "You're so stupid, I love you."

"If I'm so stupid, then why are you smiling?" I mumbled, muffled by her hug. I think she just didn't want me to see that she was crying. But, I felt a tear drop on me.

She laughed again and then took the piggy bank, gave it back to me and said, "You're my best friend, you know that, right?"

I smiled big and nodded.

"Go on, get out of here. I don't want your money." She smiled and waved me out.

I walked out and she shut the door behind me. I stood at the door for a few seconds listening. It was quiet for many seconds. Then finally, I heard the sound of her basketball being tossed at the wall. Every time I needed advice, she was there for me. Now that she needs it, even I, with my sharp mind, don't have any I can give. I wish things could be simpler. But I guess it's not as simple as having the money for both.

I went to my room and decided I would write a letter. Letter writing seems to have helped me in the past, maybe it won't let me down this time either.

Dear Sir or Madam,

My name is Samantha Lane Ferguson and I am seven years old.

I'm writing to you about my sister, Marney. She's a very talented wheelchair basketball player and she has quite a serious decision to make...

I sat at my desk writing the letter, by hand, for a very long time, so long that it became an essay, and then a story. Because this was important, I wanted to do something big for Marney and short of becoming a surgeon myself, this was my best option. I wrote and I wrote until I fell asleep at my desk. All I remember is Fred coming in to check on me and then being light as a feather for a moment before curling up in my bed fast asleep.

When I awoke, it was a bright sunny day and I knew things were going to be all right. I just had a good, cheery sort of feeling. I went to the kitchen and Marney and Fred and Jane were all already at the table talking.

"What's up?" I asked as I sat down.

Jane looked at me silently. Fred was the first to speak. "Your sister has decided."

Marney interrupted, "I'm not going to do the treatments. I'm great at wheelchair basketball. I'd rather use the money for college than an operation that we're not sure will even work."

This meant one thing and one thing only to me. She'd be going far away to college. I wouldn't see her for four years maybe longer. "Can I borrow a stamp, Jane?" I spoke up.

Jane served me breakfast and said, "Yes. What do you need it for?"

"I have a letter to mail," I responded, "for a class assignment." That was a lie. I don't usually do that but I didn't want anyone to stop me from my plan. I know what Marney said but perhaps there's a way to have the best of both worlds.

Fred looked at me kind of funny. "Do you understand what that means, Sam?"

"No sweat, Marney," I said to her as I took a big bite of scrambled eggs.

"Where would you like to go, Marney?" Fred asked.

"University of Alabama just won their third straight national championship. What do you think? Do I look like I could belong to the Crimson Tide?" Marney smiled.

"Oh, I think if they want to win a fourth, they'll have no choice but to put a uniform on you."

"Are you sure you want to go so far away, dear?" Jane asked. She said it, I was thinking it.

Marney stopped smiling. Fred put his hand over Jane's as if to tell her not to discourage Marney.

Then everybody just kept eating breakfast and no one talked the rest of the time. It was too solemn for me. I gobbled up my eggs and toast then rushed off to the mailbox to put the letter inside.

Every day for the next couple of weeks I did the same thing. Jane was getting very curious as to where all her stamps were going and I started to run out of excuses. Mailing letters everywhere didn't seem like much of a class assignment which could be graded. But, if results were anything like a grade, I was about to get an A plus.

18 CRUSHES

We're reading The Time Machine by H.G. Wells in our English class. I wish I had a time machine. I'd go back to the day of Marney's accident and tell her not to play that fateful day. I'd say, "I'm Sam, your sister from the future. You need to listen to me..."

Maybe she'd laugh. But, then again, maybe when she saw the year-ago me and the future me in the same room, she'd listen.

Cong now thinks I am avoiding him because I haven't stayed after school recently to do homework with him. I've been hard at work on my other projects. Besides, it wasn't too long ago that he was avoiding me. Boys are weird.

"Are you avoiding me?" he asked me at lunch. One thing I like about Cong, he is direct.

"No, I've just been thinking a lot."

"Oh no."

"What does that mean? 'Oh no.'"

"Whenever my mom says to my dad, 'I'm thinking,' it means my dad is in trouble. All the Chinese comes out and it gets pretty serious."

"Well, first of all, I don't speak Chinese yet and second of all, it's not about you. Okay?" I felt bad because I kind of huffed and puffed all that out and he looked defeated. "I'm sorry." I put my hand on his shoulder. "It's not you, it's me."

"Are you breaking up with me? Because I didn't even know we were going out."

I laughed. "I'm too young to date. But if we were dating, I couldn't break up with you. I like you too much."

Cong blushed. "Uh, I gotta go now. See ya in class." He got up and practically ran away. I kind of like the power I have over him. I wonder, If we had kids in twenty years would they end up being super-geniuses?

We sat in class listening to the teacher and then all of the sudden, I noticed, I was smiling and staring at the back of Cong's head. Someone else noticed too because a kid in the back hit me with a crumpled piece of paper and then laughed while pointing at me. Ugh.

Luckily before anyone noticed the reason for it, the teacher, who was feeling interrupted, stopped the class and picked on that kid, "Kenneth! Go to the principal's office for disrupting the class!"

Kenneth objected and the teacher just said, "Go!"

When all the students stopped looking at Kenneth and all of us began to look at the front of the class again towards the teacher, I noticed Cong didn't look in front. He'd been looking at me and he still was. When I noticed this, I gave him a small wave and he jolted upright in his seat a little before quickly turning to look front.

I like him. I smiled.

19 IN THE PAPERS

Every day since my letter writing campaign, I had been checking the mailbox for any responses and every day nothing happened. I was getting a little anxious. I couldn't hold Fred and Jane's questions off much longer. I'd have to say something, eventually. And what if they didn't like it? What if they got mad at me for doing what I did? What if Marney got mad at me? But, I couldn't think of the consequences now.

When Marney and I got home, I ran to the mailbox and checked it, feeling especially lucky today.

"What are you looking for, Squirt?" Marney asked.

I couldn't lie to her any longer, especially now that I was holding what I was looking for, right in my hands. It was a letter from a local college basketball scout. I opened it right away and I started to read it. Marney snatched it out of my hands and read it.

"Marney, I did it. I wrote to the colleges and asked them to come see you play."

She gave me a noogie. "I already know," Marney said.

"Ow!" I yelped and rubbed my head. "You do?"

Marney rolled into the house and I followed. "Yeah, I started getting letters a week ago from a bunch of colleges."

"You did?"

"Yeah, and who else would've done that for me?"

"You're not mad?"

"No. I'm not mad, Squirt. I know you're trying to help. But, you should leave this to me. Okay?"

"Ok, but Marney? Colleges weren't the only places I wrote to."

"Where else did you write? And why?"

I walked over to Fred's desk and I picked up the newspaper. "Looks like the paper wrote an article about you."

Marney grabbed the paper from my hands. "'Local Star Wheelchair Basketball Player Considering Spinal Surgery,'" she read. "Guess who's listed as co-writer of this article?"

"Samantha Lane Ferguson!" I yelled out my own name.

"I know you're just trying to help, Squirt, but you gotta remember. This is my life and my decision."

"I know and I'm sorry, but your decisions effect me too, Marney, and I just wanted to find colleges which were at least a little close by and have them come see you. If they knew how you played wheelchair basketball, they might help you get surgery so you can play for them or maybe they'd start a wheelchair basketball team of their own. If you go away, I'll be lost forever!"

"What would you do?" Marney asked me.

Usually, I had an answer for just about everything. But this time, I didn't know what would be right or wrong. It seemed only that there could be right and more right.

"I just want you to be able to play basketball, Marney, whenever you want, wherever you want. Without any restrictions." I said.

"You mean, without the wheelchair," she responded. "I made my choice, Sam. I'm not having the surgery because it's not a guarantee and I'd rather have wheelchair basketball than no basketball at all."

I knew she was right because she was thinking logically. But, at the same time, I wanted to be thinking positively. Maybe it wasn't at all realistic to think she could have the best of both worlds again. But, she had it all once before. Why not again? What's stopping her from being her full self again? Is it money or is it courage?

The phone rang. Marney picked it up. Her coach called her to tell her she was back on the team, her suspension was lifted.

"How'd that happen?" I asked her.

"He said, he read the article in the paper and knew that it was time I came back, that I'd suffered long enough," Marney said. "Thanks, Squirt, you pulled through for me, after all. You've got one smart noggin." She gave me a noogie again. I hate those so much.

Part Four – If You Want Something Bad Enough

20 BACK IN THE GAME

The very next day Marney was practicing again with the Challengers. With another game only a few days away, she had a lot of catching up to do.

She stayed after school, she even stayed late weekends. She had something else to prove now-that nothing was going to hold her back. Nothing.

On game day, there were people crowding out the door. Usually it's full but never like this. The gym was filled to capacity and something else, there were cameras, lots of them. I saw at least two news vans parked outside and I scanned the crowd to see if I could spot any scouts. Would they be dressed in suits? Would they be wearing a jersey from their team? Would they be incognito? I guessed that if they were there, the coach would know. So, I walked over to him and just asked, "Hey Coach, are there any scouts in the audience today?"

"Why? You expecting some?" He looked at me sarcastically. He was about to shake his head no to me when all the sudden he took a double take to the stands, "We'll I'll be..."

"What?" I asked.

"Well, it's a little strange, but yes, I see a couple," he answered.

"Coach, why would that be strange?" I asked.

But the coach got distracted. It was time to start the game and I had no more time allotted to me. He was already talking to someone else and walking away.

So, I walked away too and wondered as I looked up into the stands what was so strange about what he saw.

Suddenly, the bell sounded and the referee was throwing the ball into the air. Marney's team got it and sounding like a freight train, they rolled down the court with that ball toward the basket. Up went the ball and straight into the basket. The crowd went wild as they got their first two points.

Every time Marney got the ball, there were at least ten flashes of cameras one right after another. After several minutes of camera flashing, the other team's coach walked over to Marney's coach and poked him in the chest. They started arguing. The players on both teams got distracted and stopped playing.

The ref blew the whistle, called "Time Out!" and met with the coaches.

Finally after some shouting and pointing towards the photographers, the ref told the coaches, the game would go on with no more arguments, reporters or no reporters.

Oh boy, I did it again. I covered my face in shame.

The ref blew the whistle. I looked up to see the teams rolling into action. The ball flying down the court to an opposing player, but Marney came too fast and bore right into the other player's chair. The ball knocked against her chair and flew over to another player on Marney's team. The play was theirs to rule. Marney's teammate threw the ball back to her, she caught it and threw it into the basket for another two points.

The game continued to dazzle throughout the night. Marney led the Challengers through a great fight, as usual. The opposing team wasn't bad either. But when the game was over, the Challengers reigned champion and Marney's reputation as a star player was saved.

I ran down toward the court to talk with Marney but I couldn't get in between all the people surrounding her. I peeked through the crowd and saw Marney and several people introducing themselves to her, handing her their cards. I even heard a few times the words, "play for our school." They were the scouts. So what was so strange about them? I didn't get it.

Once again there was complete silence while we drove home.

21 GENEROUS DOCTOR MACKEY

They were regular basketball scouts," Marney said at dinner.

"What do you mean 'regular' scouts?" Fred asked.

"They don't have wheelchair basketball at those schools," Marney answered.

All of us looked at Marney. "They were all scouts from regular basketball teams? Like with legs?" I asked.

"Yeah, Sam, you should know. You invited them." Marney said.

"But, you read the letters. They said they weren't coming. And they came anyway! Do you know what this means?"

"Does it matter? I'm not going. How could I?" Marney said.

"They came, didn't they?" Fred asked. "Knowing full well they were looking at a disabled player and they came anyway."

"What do they want from me?" Marney asked confused.

"Maybe these teams are going to add wheelchair basketball to their departments, Sport. Ever thought of that?" Fred asked.

"Yeah, maybe," Marney said.

The doorbell rang. Jane went to get it and when she came back inside with an unexpected guest, Marney was even more surprised.

"Doctor Mackey?" Marney asked, "What are you doing here?"

Doctor Mackey held up the paper. "I read this and I went to your game. You're an incredible player Marney, a thrill to watch."

"I know there's a 'but,' in there somewhere," Marney said.

"But, you could be better. You could be playing like you were playing before."

Jane interrupted Dr. Mackey, "Doctor Mackey, I thought we talked about this on the phone last week, we're opting to send Marney to a college fit for the handicapped rather than paying for the surgery."

Doctor Mackey smiled, "Mrs. Ferguson, I came to a decision when I read this article. I decided I would go to Marney's game and see for myself, the girl who lives and breathes wheelchair basketball, the girl who chose to play that game disabled because she has to. When I saw her play, I decided she doesn't have to choose one over the other. Because I will fund her therapy and surgery out of my own pocket. And if I don't cure her, she can do whatever she wants, but if I do cure her, and I think I will, then she can play for any team in the nation. Anywhere she wants to go. That's why I invited the scouts."

"You invited them?" Fred and Jane asked simultaneously.

"The regular legged scouts?" I asked. "But, I thought it was me."

Doctor Mackey nodded his head. "I know about your letters, Young Lady. You made an impressive case, but until I approached them they didn't see any reason to come. I gave them that reason."

Marney had tears in her eyes and no words to speak. Fred and Jane were speechless too. But everyone watched Marney. Because it still was her choice. She could have it all-again.

Suddenly my earlier fears of Marney leaving me kicked in. Shut up fears! I really started to feel selfish and hurt and I wanted Marney to say no. But, what was I doing? What was I thinking? This is what I wanted, I wanted her to get better. Marney has always been there for me. I will be there for her no matter what. If she wants to move out of state, I will be sad and cry, but not in front of her. No way. She has to be able to do what's best for herself without her little sister getting in the way. It was time she knew that too.

"Marney?" I put my hand on her hand. "Do it. I mean, do whatever you want."

Doctor Mackey looked at me and then back to Marney, "It's going to be intense. You have to really want it."

She looked right at me and suddenly came to life. She grabbed me to her and hugged me tight. She looked at Doctor Mackey and said, "I do want it. I want to walk again."

22 GROWING UP

I was back to doing homework again after school with Cong in the library while Marney got daily physical therapy at home. I couldn't help but think how much more important her decisions are than mine. I mean, what do I do every day besides go to school? And how hard is that? I have definitely taken for granted all that I have.

"Cong?"

"Yeah?"

"I never asked you, Do you have any sisters or brothers?"

"Yeah, I have an older brother. He's a dentist. My parents are very proud of him."

"You have a brother who's grown up already?"

"Yeah, I don't think they wanted more kids after him, but when they moved to America, I think it just happened, you know, like an accident."

"I don't think you're an accident, Cong."

Cong smiled at me.

I smiled back and then asked, "What do you want to be when you grow up?"

"I'm not sure yet, but I really like video games."

"Your parents let you play video games?" I asked.

"No, but my brother sends me video games over my phone. I play them in secret."

"Wow, I didn't think you had it in you, Cong."

"What?"

"Just...I don't know. Marney would call it, a rebel spirit, I think."

"Yeah, my parents are pretty strict," he said softly. "What do you want to do when you grow up?"

"Maybe I'll be a doctor," I said with a smile.

"You're just saying that."

"No really. I think I might like it."

"Well, you better do your homework every day," Cong demanded.

"I'm here, aren't I?"

"Yeah." Then Cong got a text. His mom was waiting outside the school for him. "I have to go."

"I'll walk you out."

"No, I don't want my mom to see us together."

"But, don't your parents know we study together. That was the deal."

"Yeah, but..."

"Besides," I interrupted while shoving my books into my backpack, "you can tell them I'm going to be a doctor. That'll make them happy."

"It might," Cong said as we headed out of the library.

As we were walking out toward the front of the school, I had a strange feeling someone was watching us. I looked behind me and saw a few girls walking quickly our direction.

"Oh, please, not today, " I said.

"What?" Cong asked.

"Look Cong, I mean, don't look now, Cong, but..."

Cong started to turn his head, I grabbed it. "Don't look, I said!"

"Why not?"

"Those are the girls from the bathroom who were harrassing me. I thought I'd seen the last of them after Marney threatened them, but-"

"Your sister threatened those girls?"

"It's not how it sounds. Let's just walk faster, ok?"

Cong and I started walking faster and the girls started shouting, "Hey, wait up! Wait! We want to talk to you."

It was definitely a different tone than what I was used to coming from them. So, I stopped and turned my head to look. They were approaching quickly and then stopped right in front of us. Instead of picking me up and putting me in the trash or calling me mean names, the leader of the pack, said, "I saw you in the newspaper."

"Um, ok," I said.

"That was really cool," she said and then she and her friends walked away.

"That was weird," Cong said.

"You have no idea," I replied.

We walked outside and Cong's mom was waiting for him in a blue mini-van. My Dad was right behind her in his car. I was glad I didn't have to wait. I said goodbye to Cong and we parted ways. I hoped his mom wasn't mad at him. It's not like we did anything bad. I didn't even get to take the Sex Ed class, so I wouldn't know anything about it anyway.

23 THE LONG ROAD HOME

I got home and Marney's door was wide open. She was even singing. After several sessions of virtual reality treatment, Marney seemed to be a lot more upbeat. She spent less time alone in her room with those old game videos.

"It's like the song, 'I'm walking on sunshine.'" Marney told me. "I feel so incredible in that machine. Like I almost have my life back."

"When did they say you'll be ready for surgery?" I asked.

"I don't know, Squirt," Marney answered. "But, right now, I'm enjoying the ride. 'And don't it feel good!'" She sung out. I stood there at her doorway watching her as she shot her basketball into the hoop on her wall. She smiled and sung and I wanted to be happy for her. But I knew this easy and fun treatment wasn't going to last. Once it was over, she'd do the surgery and then the intense physical therapy. But Marney wasn't thinking of that. In a way, I didn't want to take away her happiness by reminding her either. But, she'd need a reality check soon.

And that reality check came even sooner than I'd guessed. Within a few days, Fred and Jane were called into Doctor Mackey's office to discuss the surgery and we all went down there as a family. There's another thing I realized about Jane and Fred, if we do something, we do it together.

"The treatments are going so well, I think we can do the surgery as early as next week," Doctor Mackey said.

Jane and Fred looked at each other and with some hesitation and a sigh hugged one another at the news. I'm not sure if it was a happy hug or a scared hug. But, I'm guessing it was a little of both. I didn't know what Marney was thinking but I can only imagine how uncertain it all was.

Two weeks later, Marney was scheduled for surgery. Her whole basketball team rolled into the hospital to see her go through those surgery doors. Some waited to see her when she came out, but by then, most had gone home. Only one teammate stayed.

The surgery consisted of placing some kind of electrical device right onto Marney's spinal cord. The device, when turned on, would stimulate Marney's spine and remake those connections between her legs and her brain. If it is successful, she should, with some daily physical therapy, be able to walk almost immediately.

We waited in that waiting room to hear any news, any results, anything about the surgery. Everyone drank coffee. Fred even gave me a cup. It was pretty gross. I prefer the hot chocolate. The TV was on and I could see the Simpsons was on. That's my favorite cartoon. But it was so low that I couldn't hear it. A nurse walked into the room and we all stood up with rocket speed, except for Marney's teammate of course.

The nurse looked at us and asked, "Would any of you like playing cards?"

Fred nodded his head and she gave him a set of cards. He played a round of Go Fish with Jane and Marney's friend.

I thought that game was too childish so I asked the nurse if she'd turn the TV up and when she did, I sat around and watched Homer eat donuts and drink beer, while Bart made me laugh every time he said, "Don't have a cow, Dude."

But then Doctor Mackey finally walked into the room and we knew the waiting was over. We all stopped what we were doing and stood up. Doctor Mackey looked at Jane and Fred, took off his surgical mask and said, "Marney's sleeping soundly. The surgery went well and it looks like it will be successful, but we won't know for sure until she wakes up."

"Can you give her a nudge and wake her up?" I asked.

"No, Young Lady, that would not be ideal for her. She needs to recover from the operation. When the anesthesia wears off and her body feels ready, she'll wake."

"Can we see her?" Jane asked.

"Yes, I'll have the nurse come 'round and show you to her room. I would just ask that you allow her to get the rest that her body needs."

"Ok," Fred said.

"Good," said Doctor Mackey. "I'll be back here in the morning and we'll go over the treatment plan together."

He walked out and you could see how relieved everyone was at the news. Even I had tears in my eyes.

"You softy," Fred said to me and he gave me a noogie.

"Nobody gives me a noogie except for Marney, Fred." I said to him with a snarky attitude.

"Excuse me, your highness," Fred answered. I went back to the coffee machine and bought myself a hot chocolate. It made me feel better.

The nurse finally came back and told us to follow her. She walked fast but I was right behind her. Fred and Jane held hands as they walked behind and Marney's friend was just behind me. The slick hospital floors made it easier for her to wheel around. We reached the room and the nurse gave me the shhh signal with her finger as she opened the door. I walked in quietly and took the first seat I saw. I looked at Marney. She was still sleeping. A hospital wheelchair was next to her bed.

Fred and Jane came in with Marney's friend and they sat next to Marney, right up against the bed. Jane began to stroke Marney's hair and Fred held her hand. Even with that much touchy and feely stuff Marney didn't wake up. I guess Doctor Mackey was right. She needed sleep.

Not long after that Marney's friend's mom came to pick her up. I wondered when Marney would wake and what she would say when she did. Would she remember what happened and where she was?

A few hours later, Marney woke up. I was asleep in the chair by the window when she did and was startled awake myself when I heard Jane say, with a jump, "She's awake! Fred! Marney, how are you, Sweetie?" She took one of her hands.

Fred went to Marney's side too and he took her other hand. "Hi, Sport. How ya doin'?"

Marney looked around and at first said nothing. She looked over at me and she smiled. She looked back at Fred and Jane, "What did the doctor say? Did he say it worked?"

Jane responded, "Sweetie, this is only just the beginning. You can't just get up and walk out the door right after surgery, no matter how bad you want it."

Marney looked right at Jane, "I do want it, Mom. Did he say it worked or not?"

"He said he thinks it was a success."

Marney looked at her wheelchair. "Well then," she put her arm out towards her wheelchair. Fred pushed it closer.

"Do you want to get in it, Sport?" Fred asked.

"Just leave it be," Marney answered. Fred let go of the wheelchair and backed off. Jane stood up. I stood up. We stood there, all of us, and watched and waited to see what Marney wanted to do. She pulled the wheelchair right up to the edge of the bed and then pulled her body as close to the edge of the bed as possible. Her legs weren't moving. It was all done with the strength of her arms.

"Marney," Jane tried to reason with her.

"Stop, Mom, just let me try this," Marney replied.

Marney took hold of the wheelchair like a walker. She grabbed her legs with her hands and moved them towards the floor. Her legs dangled off the bed and she started to slide toward the floor.

I started praying in my mind, Please let her stand, please let her stand, please let her stand.

By the time I thought my last thought, Marney lay on the floor. Her legs didn't hold her. She didn't move them. She didn't walk. But she cursed and cried out loud, "Damn it!"

Jane and Fred didn't get mad, they just went to the floor to help her up. Marney kept swearing and crying. Fred put Marney in the wheelchair and Marney let out her last swear word before finally kicking Fred in the calf with her right leg.

Everyone looked surprised at Marney. Fred grabbed his calf and then looked surprised at Marney, "Marney, you...kicked me."

Jane looked at Marney and let out a short fast laugh. "Honey, you kicked him!"

"Did you feel it?" I asked.

"I did," Fred said.

"Shh, Fred. Marney, Did you feel it when you kicked him?" Jane asked.

"I'm not sure," Marney replied.

Fred sighed.

My thoughts were running through my head a hundred miles a minute.

Jane smiled at Marney and hugged her. "It's ok."

"You want a hot chocolate? We can go for a stroll." Fred said to Marney.

Marney shook her head, "Just put me back in the bed, Dad, I'm tired."

Fred picked Marney up from the chair and put her back into the bed. "Anything else, Sweetie?"

Marney looked at us all, shook her head and said, "I just want to sleep."

"Come on, everybody, let's let Marney sleep," Fred said. We all gathered our things and started to leave the room.

I ran back in and kissed Marney on the cheek. It was wet with her tears. "Good night Marney."

"Good night, Squirt," she whispered back.

The next day, as promised, Doctor Mackey was back with his treatment plan. "It's perfectly normal to get some movement on the first day, even hours after surgery. It's a good sign, but it doesn't mean you can run a marathon, Marney."

Marney sat in a wheelchair in the physical therapy room with the doctor, Fred, Jane and me. It was pretty crowded. There were treadmills with people walking on top and a uniformed nurse on the side. There were weights and small rubber balls, even steps. Every single person was doing something. No one was complaining. No one was giving up. No one sat down and said I can't do it.

"I can't do it," Marney said after Doctor Mackey told her to get on the treadmill. The nurse stood by to help her get up but Marney refused to budge.

"You can do it, Marney," the doctor said. "Watch this." The doctor had a kind of remote control in his hand and he turned it on. "Do you feel anything?"

"Like what?" Marney answered. Then her toe moved.

I jumped. "Marney, your toe moved!"

"Do it again," the doctor told Marney. Then her toe moved again. "Again," the doctor said. Marney smiled and looked down as she moved it again. "The other one," said Doctor Mackey. Marney then moved the other toe. Tears began streaming down her face. Jane also wiped tears from her eyes.

"Hey, you're under remote control, Marney!" I sat down near Marney's feet and poked her toe, "Do you feel that?"

"Holy, sh--" Jane's face stopped Marney from completing the phrase, "sheesh. Yes! Yes, Squirt. I can." Every one smiled. Marney looked at Doctor Mackey, "What is that thing?"

"This is an electric impulse device. Basically the stimulator in your spine is wirelessly connected to this device. It was on last night as a test after your surgery and I can turn it on during your physical therapy and turn it off when your body is at rest."

"Why not just leave it on all the time?" Marney asked.

"Why not just stay in the Virtual Reality helmet all the time?" Doctor Mackey answered.

"Why not?!" I shouted out.

"Shhhhh!" Jane said to me.

"Like with any treatment, your body needs to learn to do this on its own. I don't want to make a substitute for your own nerves and electrical impulses. I want to remind your body and mind that it needs to use its own. We are simply recreating the ability for your body to function on its own again. Eventually, your body should reconnect itself. It should heal the injury and reconnect its own wiring, from the electrical map we're creating for it and all the while, you'll be strengthening your legs and body for when that connection happens."

"You think it will happen, Doctor Mackey?" Marney asked.

"You can train your mind and body to do anything," he said. "That's what I believe. Because I've seen it."

Marney pushed herself up off the wheelchair and with the help of the nurse standing by, she slowly moved her feet to the treadmill.

"You don't intend to put her on that thing today, do you?" Fred asked.

"Mr. Ferguson, we're not just preparing the body. We're preparing the mind." He beckoned the nurse to keep going and the nurse assisted Marney to step onto the treadmill.

Marney moved like she was carrying weights on her legs. She lifted her foot very slowly and she struggled to get it high enough, but finally stepped onto the treadmill with the first foot. With her strong arms she held tight to the handles and lifted her other foot with all her might till it landed hard on the treadmill. "It's so difficult," Marney said.

"Exercise a little control, Marney. I know everything's more heavy now, but soon, your body will remember and get used to the weight of its own limbs again." The doctor checked off some boxes on Marney's chart. "Now I want you to just lift your feet, one after the other. Just lift, nothing more."

I couldn't imagine doing this for several hours. This wasn't anything like being in the virtual reality helmet. I don't think I've ever seen Marney struggle with her body like this.

"I want you out of the chair and doing these exercises for 15 minutes three times a day," Doctor Mackey said.

Marney stayed in the hospital for two weeks. During that time there were a few reporters with cameras outside, but eventually that died down and the story I wrote for her died away too. Her coach and some players also showed up to see when she'd be back.

24 TO BE OR NOT TO BE HANDICAPPED

Soon after her hospital stay was over, she went back to school. She even played basketball in her wheelchair again. She still had to fit the physical therapy into her schedule, though.

Doctor Mackey lined up nurses to come over once in the morning before school, once in the afternoon and once at night, all for Marney. I thought that was pretty cool.

But Marney struggled to keep it together. "You can't imagine what it's like to sit in that chair all day and then go to basketball practice using only my arms, and then come home to a nurse who pushes me to stand and take steps," she opened up to us over dinner.

"You don't have to continue, if you don't want to Marney," Jane said.

"I do have to," Marney corrected her. "But, it is really confusing. It's like I'm handicapped but any time I want, I can, not be. It almost feels like I'm cheating."

25 CONG'S MOM

While Marney was struggling with her feelings after surgery, Cong was struggling with his feelings for me. Only, I didn't really understand it or know it, yet. Maybe he didn't either and that's why it was so hard for him.

In class, he wrote a poem. It was an assignment that everyone had to do, but, I know it was about me. In fact, I think the whole class knew it was about me.

"You Don't Know
by Cong Foo" Everyone laughed as he recited.

"Be quiet!" I called out.

This made Cong even more embarrassed and he blushed. But he went on...

You don't know how I feel
You don't listen to words
You make it hard to speak
You don't let me be real.

She knows
She knows me better than you
She knows
She sees me just so true

You don't know how I feel
You don't look at my face
You make it hard to say
You don't let me say

How she knows
She knows me better than..."

The kids kept laughing and interrupted throughout and it got louder and louder until he just stopped. He stopped reading his poem and folded it back up and sat down in his chair with his head down.

"Class!" The teacher finally brought order, "That's enough! Very nice Cong. A plus."

"Cong!" I tried to whisper a shout to him. "Cong!"

Cong looked back slowly.

"I really liked your poem."

He blushed and turned his head forward but I'm pretty sure I saw a smile grow on his face.

We spent lunch together again, as we did most days. I decided I would ask about the poem. "Was it about me?"

"A little bit," he replied, "but mostly about my mom."

"Oh," I said. "That's a little sad."

"Yeah, it is," he said, "but those are our ways."

"It's tradition to stomp on someone's hopes and dreams?"

"Chinese tradition is your parents' hopes and dreams are your hopes and dreams."

"Oh," I responded somberly. "But," I defended, "what if you go against those dreams and make your own dreams?"

"It's not possible."

"What do you mean? Everything's possible, Cong." I pushed him further. "This is America. You were born here. You're American. Your dreams count."

I could see he was thinking about this. I hoped I wasn't going too far, but I wanted him to know that I did see him for who he is and I appreciated him. He was my friend, a real friend and he was there when I needed him. I couldn't abandon him or allow tradition to cut our friendship. That wouldn't make sense.

Finally he said, "You're right. I shouldn't be afraid to talk to my mom. I should just tell her. I can't live her dreams anymore."

"Go Cong, " I said. "Only, don't tell her I told you all that stuff, ok?" I worried she would get mad and not let me see him again.

"Don't worry about it," he said. "I've been thinking about this a long time."

"How long?" I asked.

"Years," he said.

"But, you're nine," I replied.

"Yeah, so?"

He had a point. Look at me. I am seven and I can't stop thinking.

After school, Cong and I studied in the library, as usual and then Cong's mom came to pick him up. She actually came right into the library to get him. She stood there for quite some time before we looked up from doing our homework and when we did, she didn't look happy.

"Hi, Mrs. Foo," I said and waved.

Cong got up quickly and grabbed his backpack, "Later, Sam!"

"I thought you were gonna..." I yelled.

As they walked away together he called back, "Later..."

Then all I heard was Cong's mom speaking Chinese and Cong speaking back in Chinese. I wish I knew what they were saying.

I decided I would call Cong later and see how it went.

26 REPORT CARD DAY

At school the next day, we all got our report cards. Because I've been actually doing the work, my grades have improved quite a bit and when I say quite a bit, it means, I got all A's.

I even compared report cards with Cong. He improved in Biology, like I knew he would, because I helped him and I improved in math because he helped me. He got all A's also.

"Improved work habits," Cong read off my report card.

"Nice young man," I read off his. "Cool!" I handed his report card back to him. "Maybe your mom will like me better now."

"I talked to her last night," Cong said.

"I was going to call you and ask how it went."

"It went okay."

"But?"

"Well, she said I must be getting influenced by my American friend."

"Did you tell her I was your smart American friend? With one hundred and forty-four IQ?"

"You think I should?"

"It could help," I said.

"You're probably right."

After school, Cong and I finished our homework in the library again, then we waited outside for our parents.

For some reason, Fred and Jane didn't come to pick me up, so Cong's mom, Mrs. Foo, gave me a ride home. Cong was able to convince her I was a good girl by showing her my report card.

It was lucky, I've been doing my homework every day.

"Hi, Mrs. Foo." I sat in the front seat and Cong sat in the back. Cong's mom is funny. She speaks broken English and so when we were in the car and she asked me a question, sometimes she would speak Chinese to Cong and Cong would translate. It went something like this...

"What age you?" and then some Chinese words that I didn't know and then she looked at Cong. Cong then answered back in Chinese.

"What did she say?"

"My mom asked how old you are."

I spoke up, "I'm almost eight now!"

"I told her. You don't have to shout. She's Chinese, not deaf."

"Your mom, dad together? What they do?" Then she spoke some more Chinese words. Cong answered her back again in Chinese. Then she spoke more in Chinese and Cong answered.

"Is this all about me?" I asked.

"Unfortunately, yes," Cong said. "I asked her if we had to talk about all this."

"What did she say?"

"There's nothing else to talk about, but you."

"Mrs. Foo, you don't have to worry about me taking your son away. I'm only seven," I told her.

Cong covered his blushing face with his hand.

Cong's mom responded, "I was seven when I met Cong father."

Nothing gets past Cong's mom.

"Her parents own a construction business," Cong told her, then catching himself speaking English, he translated it into Chinese.

Cong's mom voiced her opinion with a positive sounding, "Oh!"

Then she said some words to Cong.

I turned to Cong and said, "Maybe I ought to learn Chinese."

"You better not, then she won't ever stop talking." Cong said and I stifled a giggle.

Finally we pulled up to my house. I thanked Mrs. Foo and said goodbye to Cong. "See ya in school tomorrow, Cong."

I walked into the house and Marney's door was shut. Fred and Jane were arguing in the kitchen. I walked in just quick enough to grab a snack and walk out, hopefully unnoticed, but when Fred saw me, he slapped his leg and said, "Oh damn it, I'm sorry I forgot to come get you today, Samantha."

"Who drove you home?" Jane asked.

"Cong's mom." I took a bite of an apple and looked at Jane and Fred. They didn't look like they were finished yet, so I casually walked out and went into my room.

I started unpacking my backpack and took out my report card. When I opened my door, I could hear them talking about new bills and new worries but I stepped out and walked toward the kitchen again anyway, this time yielding my super duper report card in my hand.

Fred and Jane looked at me and the room went dead silent as soon as I walked in. "Sorry, I was just..."

"Got your report card Samantha?" Jane asked.

I faked a grimace and said, "I'm really sorry, I'll try much harder." Then I held my head low and handed it to her.

Fred looked at the report card over Jane's shoulder and made a frown at me. Jane looked at him and said, "Oh stop." She turned to me and said, "Someone's been studying."

Fred smiled and hugged me. "I know this whole thing with Marney has been hard on you, too, Samantha. But, we're proud of you for getting back on track."

I was pretty proud of myself, too.

Fred signed the report card and handed it to me. "One less thing to worry about."

"How'd I get to have such a smart Cookie?" Jane asked me and gave me a kiss.

"I don't know. You wouldn't let me take the Sex Ed class, Mom."

Jane nearly flipped her lid when she heard me say it. "You just called me Mom!"

"I'm trying it on for size," I said.

Fred rubbed my head and grabbed me close for the hug. Jane hugged me too. "Dad, I can't breathe," I said.

Fred laughed, "I win! She said, 'Dad.'"

Jane butt in, "Actually, Dear, she said 'Mom' first."

They both laughed.

Funny, I've been concentrating so much on Marney and my own life that I really haven't been thinking much about Jane and Fred and what they might have been going through. They have so many adult things to worry about, like bills, something I'm lucky not to have as a kid.

Part Five – Heroes

27 MARNEY THE HERO

Journal Topic # 21 I look up to----

Dear Journal,

I look up to my sister, Marney. She is a very good person. She cares for me a lot and has always been there for me. She has always been a friend to me, especially when I didn't have any. She's super strong and very brave.

She's going to have to be even more brave because life is becoming a lot harder. I will, of course, do what I can to help.

Love,
Sam

I watched Marney struggle daily with her exercises, but she didn't give up and hardly complained. I mean, I heard a lot of swear words, and I mean a lot. But, she still lifted each foot one after another and made those small steps. The small steps became larger and larger until one day, I came home from school and Marney was waiting for us in the living room with a huge smile on her face.

"What's up, Sport?" Fred asked.

I threw my backpack into my room, ran over to Marney's room and grabbed her ball off her desk. I ran back into the living room and tossed the ball at Marney. "Think fast!"

She caught it and tossed it back. I tossed it to her again and this time she set it down.

"Hold on," she said as she started to push herself up off her wheelchair.

I looked at Fred who started to smile. Marney stood all on her own. "Cool, Marney!" I cried out.

"Wait!" she responded. And then she took steps! On her own! She struggled slightly with balance, but she did it. She then picked up the ball again and threw it to me. I threw it back to her. She caught it. Then she threw it to Fred. Fred caught it and threw it back to her.

I heard the front door open and shut. Jane had just come home. She carried groceries into the kitchen and started unpacking them. I giggled out loud as we continued to toss the ball back and forth between us three. Marney laughed and Fred laughed too.

Jane walked curiously into the hallway from the kitchen, caught a flying ball headed her way and cried out, "Oh!"

"Hi Mom," Marney said.

Jane cried, "Oh my God," handed Fred the ball and ran to hug Marney. "I'm so proud of you."

Fred surrounded Marney and Jane and gave them both a big hug. I thought I should join the party, so I hugged them all, too. We became this big hugging ball of laughter. Then Marney said, "I love you, Mom."

"I love you back," Jane responded.

"I love you, Dad," Marney said.

Fred said, "I love you too, Sport."

Then Marney said to me, "I love you too," and gave me a noogie.

"Oh geez, can we quit it with all the mushy stuff?" I said. Then Fred kissed my head and laughed out loud. "Yuck," I said.

"Feel the love, Squirt," Marney said and laughed, too.

28 SAM THE HERO

J ournal Topic #33 When I grow up, I want to be----

Dear Journal,

When I grow up, I want to be...I've been thinking about this a lot lately. This year has really shown me a direction in life that could be for me. I mean, I know I'm only 7 years old, but I think I want to go into Medicine.

I might want to be a doctor that helps people after spinal injuries, just like Doctor Mackey, the doctor helping my sister, Marney. Maybe I will be a surgeon and help people's spines connect with their brain again, so they can walk again.

It would be a pretty amazing feeling to know I helped someone heal like that.

I know I've got a long time still before I need to decide, but that's what has been going through my head recently.

Love,
Sam

We had to turn our journals back in to the English teacher today. I actually felt a little lost without my journal because it was very comforting to write in it daily. I waited and watched as many of the class turned theirs in. Even Cong got up and turned his in. I held onto mine for many minutes longer, until Ms. Harper called me up to her desk.

"Ms. Ferguson, come here and bring your journal, please."

When I walked up to Ms. Harper's desk and turned it in, Ms. Harper said to me, "Samantha, you have quite an interesting view of the world, especially your own."

"Thanks, I think," I replied.

"You should consider publishing this as a book," she said about my journal.

Cong was listening in on our conversation and he suddenly said, "I hope there's nothing about me in there!"

I turned to him and stated, "I bet there was a lot in your journal about me!" Cong turned bright red and sat back on his seat.

Ms. Harper giggled a little bit then composed herself. "Samantha, I'm quite serious. You have, potentially, a great story here and a way to make some money for yourself and your family, plus save up for college, medical school, whatever you want."

That got my attention, because even with Doctor Mackey paying for Marney's treatment, Fred and Jane were still behind on the bills. I decided that maybe Ms. Harper was right.

After class, Cong and I walked to lunch together and he asked me, "Are you really going to become a doctor?"

"Maybe," I said. "Maybe a writer, too."

"I think I'll just tell my mom you're going to become a doctor."

I laughed, "Ok, Cong, tell her what you want."

"Trust me, it's better that I do."

We laughed.

Cong is my best friend. I don't know if he is really going to be my boyfriend, but for right now, I like that we're just friends with a little mystery on the side.

"So, what are you going to be when you grow up?" I asked him. "You never told me."

"I decided I'm going to design video games."

"Did you tell your mom yet?"

"No, I figured I would wait until I tell her you're going to be a doctor. That way, she'll know we'll be ok." He blushed a little as he waited for me to respond.

"You do still remember that I'm only seven, right, Cong?"

"Yes, and you remember my mom said she met my dad when they were seven?"

I laughed to cover up my blushing face and he joined in.

29 MOM & DAD THE HEROES

J ane and Fred, my mom and dad, pulled up to the school to pick me up on the last day of school. I got into the car and asked, "Where's Marney?"

"We're going to go get her, now," my mom responded.

Fred smiled at me.

"What's the big mystery?" I asked.

"It's a surprise," Fred stated.

"I realize that, Dad." I answered.

"Wow, I don't know how I'm going to get used to this," he replied.

"Used to what?" I asked.

"Used to you calling me Dad," he replied. "It's like some miracle. Either that or some aliens came down and switched you out. Which one is it?"

"Dad!" I laughed. "I am me."

Dad laughed, too.

The car started slowing down as we neared our destination. Mom was eagerly looking about. Dad parked the car and we all got out.

"Fred, there she is!" Mom stated enthusiastically. She pointed to a basketball court where Marney was standing at the free throw line and shooting basket after basket.

Mom started running, so I started running and Dad did, too. We ran all the way to the basketball court and were out of breath by the time we reached Marney.

"You guys are out of shape!" she said loudly and threw another two-point shot.

The ball bounced towards Dad and he dribbled and tossed to Marney. Marney made the shot, it rebounded and she caught it and threw it to me. I ran up to the basket and threw it underhanded. It landed on top of the rim and I could hear everyone eagerly shouting, "Go in, go in!" as it rounded the rim and finally plop, it went in. "Yay!" they all cheered for me.

We played a long time that night, all together, as a family-Mom, Dad, Marney and me. I told Mom and Dad all about what Ms. Harper said and about the book I'm going to write. "It'll help pay the bills," I said, "and if there's any money left over, then when Marney goes to school, I can go visit her."

Marney made a 3-point shot and walked toward me. "I'd really like that, Squirt."

She gave me a huge hug. Mom and Dad joined in and Dad said, "We're so proud of you Girls."

Our family hugs last forever-geez! "Dad, I can't breathe," I said as everyone laughed.

The End.

ABOUT THE AUTHOR

Dear Reader,

I was born in Arlington, Massachusetts. I grew up in Silverlake, California, with a big energetic and happy family of five brothers and one sister.

My interest in writing started because of my interest in reading. My most beloved childhood books were "The Wizard Children of Finn" by Mary Tannen and "The Witch of Blackbird Pond" by Elizabeth George Speare.

Later it was Stephen King's deliciously horrifying pages that occupied my interests. A recommendation to HP Lovecraft got me hooked to his short horror stories. Then I fell in love with the science-fiction of Robert Heinlein and the classics of William Somerset Maugham.

These are the authors that made me want to be a writer. These are the authors I felt should have been on the top of my reading list in school. I was disappointed by many of those books which we were forced to read. Some were brilliant, others fell short of my expectations.

I recall that in the 6th grade we were taught how to write and bind children's books and I wrote a book called Jessica and the 3 Magic Ghosts. I also did another called The Butterfly and the Ladybug, which at 15 years old, I tried to publish. That was my first taste of disappointment with something called a "rejection letter."

In junior high school, I became both an actor and a director. I was taught through experience how to direct my fellow students and act with them in Shakespeare, Improvisation and all sorts of pieces. I also took Speech which continued my training in writing and I competed in many speaking and acting competitions.

My love of writing goes hand-in-hand with my love of people, languages and cultures. In high school, I studied German and Spanish. At fifteen, I got a scholarship for a summer exchange program. I lived in Berg, Germany for two months, and that short span of time expanded my viewpoint of the world. My interest in Germany and travel had become so intense that I became industrious and worked hard baking cookies and cakes to sell, working a part time job and asking for donations to pay for another exchange.

Having earned enough money during my last high school year, I returned to Germany as an exchange student for an entire year. I lived in the gracious little town of Oberharmersbach in the heart of the Black Forest for a month of language camp then I moved north to the former-German-Democratic-Republic city of Stralsund where I attended school. The city scared me at first, looking like the war had been just yesterday. My host parents there had spent practically their whole lives behind the wall of the GDR (German Democratic Republic) and decided they would make up for lost time. They traveled extensively and when I arrived, they took me to Sweden, Denmark, Norway and Poland. I discovered there was another world out there with amazing places and people.

After leaving Germany, I returned to Los Angeles and chose to work for my church full-time. I had heard the stories of the former East Germany and seen wartime ruins, I wanted to help people. I feel that what I learned in church about religion, about people and about responsibility and ethics was something no other experience could have given me and I'm blessed to be able to have had that. I continued to travel back and forth from Europe and am addicted to the beauty of its lands and people.

I held many jobs over the years and although some involved Art, most did not. I had only been working on my writing and acting part time and I decided I had strayed from my passion for too long.

I knew the role of the artist could influence society in a positive and big way. I wanted to use my gift, my experiences and my insight as a creative outlet to help people. I got involved with a local theater and began acting. I educated myself in the entertainment business by attending workshops and reading books. I subscribed to "VARIETY, an informative newspaper for Hollywood creative people."

One 3 a.m. morning, I got an inspiration and wrote the dark comedic play, "An Act of God." I presented it to the producers at a theater I'd been acting in, and we planned auditions to take place the next month. I ran the auditions, rehearsals and performances (sold-out shows) and fell in love with directing.

My love of writing was even stronger and I kept creating. I presented my romantic office comedy, "Brown Eyed Girls" to another full house. I was motivated! I wrote daily. I now wanted to be a director. I began reading screenplays and books about screenplay writing. I paid close attention to movies and educated myself. I turned my novel I had started when I was twenty years old, into my screenplay, "Isabella's Letters.

I continued to write for the theater. I wrote and directed, "The Trial of Abraham" a court drama and "Uninvited" a psychological thriller and a psychological drama, "Secrets." I filmed three shorts, derived from my plays, "Uninvited", "An Act of God" and "Brown Eyed Girls." It was both nerve wrecking and exhilarating. I played the lead role of a German woman named, Marion, in the film, "Begleiter" (which means Companion, in English) by Dan Margules. I was thrilled that I got to use my foreign language skills and accent. We received rave reviews and won several film festivals. I cast a short film called, Being In Sync, about a thirty-something boyband has-been who's sick of his telemarketing job and wants to get the band back together. I met with many talented actors and finally we nailed the perfect ones down. The premiere was a big success.

Since then, I've written many more scripts, short stories and poetry and acted in many more short films. I also have produced music videos, public service announcements and all sorts of comedy webisodes. I'm currently working on a new script, a new book and a feature film. Every day I get to do this, I smile because I am happy creating imaginary worlds for you and other readers and audiences of film and tv.

My wish for you is that you look at your life with enthusiasm and know that your goals are attainable, meaning, you <u>can</u> win! Trust in yourself and take those first few steps, get on your path to success in whatever field you love and go for it. Whether it's sports, health, acting, singing, dancing or designing buildings, whatever it is, you can win. You can be anything if you just dare to dream it. You can make it happen.

All my best,

Aleisha Gore

AUTHOR'S GLOSSARY

Acupuncturist –Chinese medicine that involves pricking the skin or tissues with needles, used to relieve pain.

Affiliate –Attach or connect oneself to or with someone or something.

Analogies –Comparison of something with something else (like when Marney compares life to a basketball game)

Agility -The ability of a person or animal to move quickly and with beauty.

Albino –A person without pigment in their skin and so they have very white skin, white hair and pink eyes.

Anesthesia –Injection of drugs into a patient before surgery.

Bart Simpson -A fictional main character in the animated TV series The Simpsons, known for his sarcastic witty remarks.

Borderline –Almost reaching a certain point.

Candidate -A person who qualifies for a certain surgery or medical procedure.

Crimson Tide –The Team name of the University of Alabama.

Crystal People –People who use "healing crystals" for "energy medicine."

Device-A thing made for a specific purpose, a machine.

Disperse –To spread over a large area or to leave an area.

Eavesdropping –Secretly listening to private conversation.

Expo –A large exhibition.

Favoritism –The act of giving unfair treatment to one person or group over another.

Fervently –With a passion or intense feeling.

Flirted –Playfully trying to attract someone's attention.

Flustered –To be confused.

Grimace –A facial expression of disapproval or disgust.

Gritted –Clenched the teeth tightly.

Guru –Someone who is regarded as having great knowledge.

Hallucinating –Seeing something that's not necessarily there.

Horrid –Very unpleasant or disagreeable.

Impulse –A strong urge to do something.

Incognito –Taking on a fake identity. Hiding.

Instinctively –Arising from impulse, without thinking, just knowing.

Ironic –Opposite of or different from the normal expectations and thus causing amusement.

Kombucha –Fermented tea drunk for medicinal purpose, having very little alcohol in it.

Mimicked –Imitating someone or something in their actions or words.

Mongo –From the word: Humongous, and taken from the movie "Blazing Saddles" to show this character is large and dumb.

Munchkin –From the Wizard of Oz to indicate a small person, used as a mean word in this book.

Nimble –Quick.

Noogie –A hard poke or grind with the knuckles on one's head.

Nurse Practitioner –An advanced educated Nurse who has a Master or Doctorate Degree in Nursing.

Opt Out-To choose not to participate in something.

Overexert –To go beyond one's strength while exercising or playing sports.

Paralyzed –Not able to move either fully or partially.

Paraplegic –A person who is paralyzed from the waist down.

Precision –The quality of being exact or precise.

Prudish –Excessively proper or modest in speech or dress or actions.

Queasy –Feeling sick to one's stomach.

Retorted –Replied, answered in a sharp or angry way.

Riff-raff –A negative word meaning undesirable people.

Rival –A person or team who's competing against another.

Self-censorship –To stop oneself from saying or writing something.

Seventh Circle of Hell –Referring to a book Dante's Inferno, in which hell had levels and the 7th was for the violent people.

(The) Simpsons –A very popular comedy cartoon on TV.

Spectators –People who watch, usually sports, but can be used in other ways.

Virtual Reality –Seemingly real but computer generated simulation of real life.

Wordsmith —A poetic way of saying someone who is good with writing or words.

Youtube —A website used to upload and show videos of just about anything from sports games to home videos.

3NMS000034863E

14807961R00091

Made in the USA
Charleston, SC
02 October 2012